A MAGICAL INTERLUDE

Finally, Hazelforth took a deep breath, squared his shoulders, and took her by the hand. "Come here, Cat. Stand where I can see you. You are especially beautiful tonight, you know. But then you are always beautiful."

Dazed, Cat looked up at him in the candlelight. His eyes were dark with emotion. "I remember the day I first saw you, there in the sacristy," he went on, his voice coming softly to her through the semidarkness. "Not only beautiful, but so very much yourself, so very different from anyone I had ever met before. In spite of your tempers, in spite of the fact that you could barely tolerate my presence—yes, I knew it well—I was compelled to seek you out. I could not help myself then. Nor can I now."

Cat had little time to reflect on this declaration, for she almost immediately found herself enveloped in Hazelforth's arms as his lips urgently sought hers. She wondered for a fleeting second why she had no inclination at all to struggle in this embrace, and then lost track of everything except her rushing senses. . .

An
Impetuous Miss
Mary Chase Comstock

ZEBRA BOOKS
KENSINGTON PUBLISHING CORP.

For my sister, Sue McPherson,
who gave me time and
a place to write.

ZEBRA BOOKS

are published by

Kensington Publishing Corp.
475 Park Avenue South
New York, NY 10016

First Printing: January 1993

Printed in the United States of America

Chapter One

Cat Mansard stifled an irritated sigh as her cousin held up one more piece of lacy finery for her admiration. Weddings and trousseaux were not terribly interesting, she reflected, particularly if they were not one's own. Cat was certainly not jealous of her cousin's good fortune. As far as she was concerned, Cecily was welcome to John Winters and his fortune. John was wealthy, handsome, kind . . . and altogether dull. Fortunately, however, he made an ideal match for Cecily Keating: she was terribly pretty and sweet, but no prodigy. On the other hand, those who knew Catherine Mansard had pronounced her temper uncertain, her manners unconventional, and her sharp wit somewhat daunting in a woman.

"You will have a Season in London, of course," Cecily was saying, "and before long I shall know scads of people to introduce you to, and they will help us find an eligible bachelor for you."

"Not likely," returned Cat, smoothing the folds of a delicate ecru nightgown. "In the first place,

I've no intention of throwing in my lot with that artificial game they call the London Season. Why they don't call it 'daughters on the auction block' and have done with it, I cannot guess. And second, it is hardly likely that anyone would assist a new acquaintance in search of introductions, for there's not a person on the globe who isn't sharp on the lookout for husbands for their own eight or nine deserving nieces or cousins. Besides, Cecily, those who are eligible have turned out to be such fools! Remember Bath?! Great heavens, I vow I thought I'd perish if we had to spend another week breathing the same air as those foppish buffoons!"

"You judged them too harshly, Cat. We met some perfectly agreeable young men in Bath. After all, I met John in Bath! *You* scared them off with all of your books and quotations—not to mention the occasional fit of bad temper! I vow there must be nothing you like better than to shock an entire room into silence." Cecily shook her golden curls and posed in front of the mirror with her wedding veil before turning to face her cousin accusingly. "If you're not careful, Cat Mansard, you'll live out your days as the Spinster of Sparrowell Hall."

"There are worse things than spinsterhood," Cat remarked as she looked at their two reflections in the mirror, her own dark features and angular face contrasting sharply with Cecily's golden, more rounded beauty. "I have no intention of playing predator or victim in London or anywhere else.

I've got sufficient fortune to last me two lifetimes, and a well-stocked library besides. I shall leave them both to your future children, of course, so it's in your best interests to leave me in the country with none but Parson Tweedle for temptation. I shall be very happy, very eccentric and, above all, mistress of my fate!"

"Gammon!" Cecily exclaimed. "I pray you do not take me for a brainless bumble, Cat. There is not a female in the world who does not long for love and *you,* I warrant, are no exception, for all you wish to appear so!" Then, she smiled at Cat with a mysterious expression, "I have quite different plans for you, my dear. Before you know it, I shall have you following me down the aisle!"

What on earth was Cecily up to now? She had tried her hand at matchmaking before, always with disastrous results. Cat grimaced at the memory of several well-intentioned, bland young men who had retreated from her unconventional behavior and conversation in hasty confusion. But before Cat could pursue Cecily's comment further, they were interrupted by a knock at the door as Felicia, who had served as the girls' maid for the last three years, breezed into the chamber with a perfunctory curtsy.

"Miss Cat, there's Mr. Snagworth downstairs to see you about some estate business as your uncle's not in. He's waiting for you in the library."

Casting her cousin a warning look, Cat availed herself of this opportunity to escape further perusal of the wedding finery. Outside the door, she was met with an enthusiastic greeting from her Aberdeen terriers, Caesar and Brutus, who had been scratching and whining at the chamber door with admirable persistence for the last half hour. The two mischievous villains had been banished from Cecily's chamber after having wrought havoc with her trousseau on at least one occasion. Cat had found their antics exceedingly amusing; this afternoon, however, she noted the tears of frustration rising in her cousin's eyes as the dogs burrowed their wet noses into a stack of lavender-scented linens. Reluctantly, their mistress had shooed them out. Now, they bounced energetically about her feet as she made her way down the magnificent central staircase past the portraits of her ancestors, all of whom seemed to be frowning at her with decided disdain. She had a good idea what they would be thinking, were they alive. A young lady meeting with the estate manager! Most indecorous! She smiled and flounced past them.

Entering the library, Cat looked about her. There was no sign of Snagworth, but perhaps he had stepped out to enjoy the brightness of the day. The French doors to the adjoining walled garden were open, letting in the sunshine and scent of new roses. The library was Cat's favorite room, not only because of its beauty, rich with Oriental carpets and mahogany shelves lined with well-loved volumes. This was the room in which Cat had spent so many quiet hours with her grandmother, healing the wound of her parents' untimely deaths when Cat was ten.

Gran had undertaken Cat's rearing with enthusiasm and imagination. Although she had loved her son and daughter-in-law, she had always found them desperately conventional and did all she could to foster a sense of social responsibility and intellectual curiosity in her grand-daughter. Together, Cat and Gran had read and talked about books and issues of the day. "Don't hide your brains," Gran had told her often. "A man who's worth anything wants a woman with a brain, not a simpering smile. Your grandfather did."

Those years with Gran had been all too short, however. When Gran died five years later, Cat wondered if the void left by her death could ever be filled. Of course, Uncle Martin and Aunt Leah had come to Sparrowell Hall to be with Cat and direct the affairs of the estate. They were good people, pleasant people, who had gallantly shouldered the task of reining in their unpredictable, outspoken niece. She and her cousin Cecily had become fast friends as well, but the moods and tirades that Gran had understood and smoothed over often left Cat's other relations in puzzled silence.

After several fruitless months they had philosophically and wearily given up their endeavors. During the years that followed, they had found several opportunities to be thankful that Cat had sufficient fortune and beauty to offset her liabilities when the time came for her to marry. All things considered, however, the five years until Cat attained her majority had provided them with more joy than sorrow.

Cecily's forthcoming marriage coincided neatly with Cat's coming of age. She would celebrate her twentieth birthday at the end of the week, come into her inheritance, and Aunt Leah and Uncle Martin, now suddenly relieved of their responsibilities, looked forward anxiously to the time when they could return to their own small estate in the Lake District. When Cat had announced several months earlier that she neither wanted nor needed their help in running the estate, she had met with embarrassingly little protest from her guardians. Immediately, Uncle Martin had taken pains to acquaint her with the duties she would soon assume. Indeed, ever since her announcement, both he and her aunt had worn the look of prisoners who couldn't quite believe the good fortune of a sudden and early reprieve.

Before agreeing to the plan, however, her guardians had insisted that Cat introduce some sort of older, reliable companion to Sparrowell for the sake of propriety. This was easily acceded to, for, while Cat looked forward to her independence, she did not really wish for the isolation which she would be forced to endure without such companionship. Without proper chaperonage, even Cat recognized that, as an unmarried lady of position, she could neither call nor undertake visits of any length. Hence, Cat considered herself fortunate indeed in being able to convince her former governess, Miss Eveline Bartlett, to undertake the role of companion. While Cat had been the guilty author of the few moments of anger Miss Bartlett had experienced in life, Cat had always sensed a sympathy between them and hoped they could be friends.

Cat made her way through the library and looked out into the little garden. There, behind a camellia bush, she spied Snagworth engaged in some curious, and obviously covert, activity by the wall. "Snagworth!" she called out. "Whatever are you about?"

"Eh, what's that?!" he stammered, brushing his hands off on his waistcoat as he stepped into the sunlight. He was a bent little man whose red face bespoke an appetite for spirits, but a good manager by all accounts. "Ah, Miss Catherine, you're a prompt one, ain't you! Not like some young folks who'd leave a poor auld man waiting. Well, you ask yourself," he laughed nervously, "what's auld Snagworth doing in the garden? Well, you're a smart one indeed and caught me at a little act of charity. Feeding the squirrels I was. Squirrels are very dear creatures, ain't they? Nature's little gift, I always say."

Cat looked at him closely. Uncle Martin had always spoken highly of Snagworth and vowed the man had proved his worth many times in the two years since he had been engaged, but this sudden interest in the well-being of squirrels took her aback. Dear creatures indeed! Only a month ago, she had heard him refer to squirrels as vermin. "Rats with bushy tails," he had called them. What on earth could be behind this turn around, she

11

wondered?

"Well, Miss Catherine, just a few estate items, just a few papers for you to sign, as your uncle's engaged. Nothing difficult. I won't be taking you from the wedding plans for long. I know how this business turns a girl's head. And soon we'll be hearing the same sweet bells for you. Never a doubt about it."

If Snagworth had been dealing with her longer, Cat thought, he would have known the folly of his words. Thus far, however, his dealings had been almost entirely with Uncle Martin. Lately, she had gradually begun to assume responsibility, but Uncle Martin's pacifying presence had helped her to hold her temper in check. Once her guardians had made their departure, Snagworth would learn about her quickly enough. She smiled as she envisioned the scene. Cat glanced quickly over the documents, a purchase of supplies and a change of tenancy for one of the families who farmed on the estate. Nothing of any consequence, she thought as she signed.

"Well done, well done," chortled Snagworth condescendingly, rocking back and forth on his heels and smiling. "We'll get on just fine then, Miss Catherine. There'll be no problems with the estate at all. Just trust auld Snagworth and all will be well. All will be well indeed."

So, Cat sniffed to herself, Snagworth thought it was a fine accomplishment for a woman to be able to sign a few papers? She could hardly wait to see his surprise when he discovered that, after the to-do surrounding Cecily's wedding subsided, she intended to sit down with him and go over all of the estate books in detail, no matter how long it took. This news could wait, however. As Snagworth took his leave, bowing his way out of the room, Cat indulged in the uncharitable pleasure of imagining the discomfiture he would meet in the next several weeks.

The thousand-odd last minute preparations for the next day's nuptials went late into the evening and it was with gratitude that Cat finally curled into the crisp lavender scent of her feather bed. Sleep did not come immediately, but when it did, her dreams were disconcerting, plagued with visions of Snagworth kneeling before her saying, "Ah, Miss Catherine, my dearest love, say you'll be mine and I'll dress you from head to toe in the softest of squirrel skins." In her sleep, Cat shuddered, frowned, and turned over.

Chapter Two

The day of the wedding dawned clear, blue, and full of good portents, with a refreshing cool breeze blowing in from the nearby seashore. Cecily would be a lovely bride, Cat thought contentedly as she looked out over the green morning hillsides, and she was sure that the environs of Sparrowell Hall would not suffer in comparison to any other setting. Cecily and her parents, whose fortune was adequate but by no means lavish, had decided against a fashionable ceremony in London. Moreover, since so much of Cecily's young adulthood had been spent at Sparrowell, she felt far more comfortable being wed in the village church than returning to her own district.

John Winters' family had arrived several days earlier and Cat was glad that she'd been able to lodge his parents and sundry aunts, uncles, and cousins in one of the larger houses on the estate which conveniently happened to be vacant. This provided both families with a degree of privacy so necessary to the amicable beginning of a close association, as well as opportunity for the hectic wedding preparations to be carried out without too much interruption or superfluous advice.

Cat's responsibilities began almost at dawn as she directed the arrangement of the dining room and formal salons for the festivities that would follow the ceremony. Flowers had been gathered, not only from the conservatory, but from the gardens and hillsides which were blossoming profusely in the first real warmth of the season. Before long, every available surface was piled with fragrant branches of mock orange, pale rosebuds, and lilies of every description. These had to be arranged upon the tables, around the cake, woven through candelabra and twined up the banisters of the central hallway while still fresh. In the gardens, workmen were busily setting up the green-and-white-striped pavilions where the wedding guests would take their tea after the ceremony. Meanwhile, Uncle Martin anxiously conferred with Chumley, the butler, about the chilling of champagne and mixing of punch.

It was nearly nine o'clock by the time these arrangements had been completed and Cat took a moment to look in on Cecily before she began her own toilette. As she made her way down the paneled hallway she hastened her steps, for a confused mélange of wails and exclamations issued alarmingly from Cecily's chamber. There, in the midst of a great confusion of lace, flowers, chambermaids and Aunt Leah, stood Cecily still dressed only in her chemise.

"Oh, Cat," Cecily cried plaintively as she looked up to see her cousin. "Thank heavens you're finally up. I don't know what to do first and neither does Mother. I can't find anything. Not my pearl earbobs, not my gloves, not my prayer book. I know they were here yesterday . . ."

While Cat found the sight of the customarily composed Cecily and her quiet, unassuming mother struggling in a tangle of prenuptial jitters most diverting, she managed to conceal her amusement. "Now, Aunt Leah, you sit over here out of the way for just a moment. Here are your gloves and prayer book right under your veil where we put them last night, Cecily. Now take a look in the mirror for just a moment . . ."

"Oh, Cat," she wailed, "You must know I've no time for that, I . . . oh, my earbobs!"

"Yes, they're in your ears, you goose. Now what's to be done first? Have you had tea yet?"

"Oh, how beastly! I couldn't. Not this morning!" Cecily protested.

"Well, I certainly could, and it looks as if you and Aunt Leah had better join me unless you feel that the service would be better accompanied by curious noises from your tummy than the pumping of the organ. In any case, between the two, we would never be able to hear John say 'I do' and that, of course, is of the utmost importance." Then Cat turned to a maid and said, "Run and tell Cook we shall need a pot of strong tea and some scones, if she has any. Nothing too rich this morning. All right, Cecily, sit here out of the way. Now, then, let's arrange all of your finery in the order you'll need it . . ."

When Cat was finally able to return to her chamber to don her own wedding apparel, she did so secure in the knowledge that Cecily would be the most beautiful bride the county had ever seen. Her golden hair had been braided and coiled with white roses and sprigs of lavender. From this arrangement, a few flaxen tresses curled down onto her white shoulders. The dress itself was reminiscent of a white rose with all its layers of snowy tulle and lace. Cecily was perfect, from the yards of misty veiling to her little satin slippers, and Cat hoped that John would sufficiently appreciate the vision they had toiled to create.

In her own chamber, Cat turned with less satisfaction to her image in the mirror. She wondered without much hope whether Felicia would be able to work some miracle with her disorderly dark curls. In any case, there wouldn't be a great deal of time, for the carriages were due to depart for the chapel in less than two hours. Cat sighed in resignation at the likelihood that, standing next to Cecily's glowing beauty, it was altogether doubtful whether anyone would notice if she had hair at all.

"Felicia!" Cat called sweetly down the hallway. "I have a challenge for you!" Felicia, who had struggled on this battleground before, with varying degrees of success, fleetingly considered throwing herself from the nearest tower window. Nevertheless, she pushed up her sleeves and approached her mistress's tangled locks with a look of fierce determination. By the time the valiant maid had completed her task, the poor thing was on the verge of nervous exhaustion, but owned that Cat looked quite presentable.

"You must have used every hair pin in four counties," Cat exclaimed. "I shall be in luck indeed if I am not mistaken for a hedgehog!" She regarded herself critically in the mirror. At least everything looked and felt secure — for the moment. Lavender and baby's breath peeked coyly out from her curls. The charming effect was a little disconcerting, and Cat charitably hoped that none of the guests naively mistook her for the sweet creature she now appeared to be. Given the state of her nerves, the result might be disastrous. She shook herself from these musings, however, and set about completing her toilette. All that remained was to slip into her gown and wait for Felicia to assist her with the tapes.

The dress was styled on a more simple pattern

than the bride's, but still had more ruffles and embroidery than anything Cat, who favored more classic styles, had ever worn before. It was lilac silk with small flowers of a deeper shade embroidered on it. Layers of lace and lilac ribbon fell in cascades at the elbow and bodice. Around her throat, Cat tied a moss green velvet ribbon from which hung a filigreed amethyst drop that had once been her grandmother's.

When Cat finally turned to meet her reflection she did so with some satisfaction. In spite of her reputation for being bookish, Cat enjoyed her appearance, which had become increasingly dramatic as she grew taller and her figure matured in the last two or three years. Her green eyes turned up at the corners as she smiled, and she realized that, as Cecily had often remarked, she did look very much like a pretty cat who had just figured out how to corner a tempting mouse.

"That's a job and a half I've done today, Miss Cat, but I daresay you look as good as Miss Cecily!" exclaimed Felicia, who felt her labors earned her a proprietary interest in her mistress's appearance.

"Yes, I suppose I shall do all right," Cat concurred languidly, feigning boredom. Felicia merely rolled her eyes and sighed at the mistress she adored but would never understand.

Downstairs, the air was thick with the combined agitation of Cecily and Aunt Leah. The bride paced back and forth wringing her hands as her mother followed, seemingly in tow as she attempted to straighten Cecily's veil and retie her satin sash.

"She's already got the gentleman, Aunt Leah," Cat called as she descended the stairs, "but she won't if we keep him waiting at the altar!" At that, Uncle Martin tut-tutted and shooed the distraught pair toward the carriage which would take them the short distance to the church.

Once the party was securely settled in the carriage, Aunt Leah collapsed into exhausted catatonia, and Uncle Martin, not one to be effusive, surveyed his daughter and niece with pleasure and told them they were looking well. Cecily smiled as she, too, regarded Cat in secret satisfaction and squeezed her hand. Perhaps her little plot would work after all.

It was with some degree of astonishment that Cat watched Cecily sail through the rest of her wedding day with composure and serenity. Apparently the perfection of the ceremony itself, and perhaps the sentiments it celebrated, had eliminated all the disorder and jangled nerves of the morning hours, for Cecily and John did indeed make a storybook bride and groom.

Surprisingly, it was Cat herself who spent the remainder of the day in a turmoil of emotions. Just before the ceremony was to begin, Cecily had suddenly grasped her cousin by the arm. "Oh, Cat, I almost forgot! I wanted John to wear a rose from my bouquet in his buttonhole! I know you must think I'm a sentimental fool, but would you take this to him for me? I shall have Papa tell the organist to play another hymn, so you will have plenty of time."

Overcoming her exasperation with the excesses of young lovers, Cat took the flower and proceeded with haste to the sacristy door. There she found John pacing back and forth closely followed by a hovering Parson Tweedle, whose nervous complaints at such functions were well known. At the window seat lounged a tall blond man, watching with amused indolence the distress of his companions. His very composure in such a scene annoyed Cat, who hurried in and caught John's coattail as he sailed by.

"Be still half a moment while I fix this flower, John. It comes fresh from Cecily's bouquet, a token of her dearest love!" Cat succeeded in smiling prettily as she delivered this little speech, although John looked at her with some suspicion. He had seen enough of her in various moods over the last several months to distrust her present tone. However, he soon recollected himself and took her by the arm.

"I say, I'm glad you've come, Cat. May I present my cousin, Charles Hazelforth. He only just arrived last night and he will be standing up with me today. Hazelforth, this is Cecily's

21

cousin, Miss Catherine Mansard."

With some sudden interest, Hazelforth had roused himself from his perch on her entry and now bent briefly over Cat's hand, drawling smoothly, "Your servant, Miss Mansard. John is clearly fortunate in his new family as well as in his bride."

"That is my opinion as well," Cat returned with an icy sweetness, for the glibness of Hazelforth's compliment had ruffled her already much tested humor. It was her confirmed conviction that much of the falseness of the society she scorned was characterized by such conventions. "We shall see in time if Cecily is likewise blessed, I suppose. Though John is certainly a paragon among men, my estimation of his family is still at a formative stage."

Cat had considered this an appropriate set-down, and was therefore dismayed when Mr. Hazelforth merely threw back his head and laughed heartily. Nothing could have ruffled her more, for, while she was ordinarily good-natured, she despised any mirth at her expense. As the color rose to her cheeks, she turned abruptly and hurried away to take her place in the processional. Just outside the sacristy door, however, she discovered that the silk tie on one of her slippers had come loose and, as she stooped to retie it, she heard Mr. Hazelforth's voice from the open window above her head.

"Great heavens, John, however did such a

creature find her way into sweet little Cecily's family? I vow I expected her to bite me any minute!"

"Oh, that's just Cat's manner," John replied affably. "I swear I was half afraid to be in the same room with her for months when I first knew Cecily. But Cat's all right, really, if she's in a good mood and not reading. If you interrupt her in the middle of a book, there's deuce all to pay."

"Really? And is she held rapt by these tiresome French novels as half society is these days?"

"Well, you know I'm not much for the books," John returned good-naturedly, "but I believe her taste pretty much runs the gamut. Burns and Burney, Richardson and Radcliffe, Cowper and the crew."

"A lady scholar! Heaven preserve us!" Hazelforth exclaimed in tones of mock horror. "Well, I suppose she must find some way to occupy her time, as she's clearly not concerned about her reception in society."

"No, I suppose our Cat is somewhat eccentric, but she's determined not to marry anyhow, so I expect it's well enough."

"She's certainly pretty enough for the London set, but within a month no house would receive her unless she behaves differently from how she just did. She'd have to be as rich as Croesus to tempt a member of the *ton*," Hazelforth went on speculatively.

"She very nearly is," replied John. "Quite likely the richest heiress in three counties, so even though she says she'll have none of London, I expect she'll continue to have offers. Watching these wags get their comeuppance is deuced good sport, though. I say, Charles, you seem uncommonly interested in our Cat. Never tell me you're thinking of having your measurements taken for the old leg shackles?"

"I assure you, John," came the quick reply, "I shall allow you to enjoy that blissful state all by yourself. Your Miss Mansard is quite a picture, but I hope you do not imagine that, after all this time, I should at last surrender my heart to *her* tender mercies."

At this, Cat felt that she had heard quite enough for the present and hurried away with their amused laughter at her heels. Odious men! They always brought out the worst in her. Oh, why couldn't she just have been quiet and kept her misanthropic thoughts to herself, she wondered in agitation? She hoped with some contrition, though, that her loose tongue and reckless manners would not hurt Cecily's reception in her new family. It was frustrating, however, to be reminded that merely speaking her mind was the source of either shocked dismay or, far worse, disdainful amusement.

"Thank you so much, Cat," Cecily beamed at her when she had finally made her way back. "I feel much better now. Did you meet Mr. Hazelforth?"

"I did indeed," Cat fumed. "Annoying creature!"

"Why Cat! Whatever is the matter?" Cecily asked, her eyes wide with concern.

"Tut tut, girls," Uncle Martin broke in hastily, "It's time to begin."

It was all Cat could do in the seconds that remained to compose her countenance, if not her spirits, to avoid looking like a storm cloud as she preceded Cecily down the aisle. As the organist began to play a Handel largo, Cat prodded forward the three little girls in white dresses who were to scatter rose petals and lavender before them; then she gave Cecily's hand a quick squeeze and began down the aisle herself.

That pathway seemed suddenly miles long and indeed presented an exercise in self-control. At the foot of the altar stood John, with whom she was now quite out of charity, as well as his odious cousin, who was smiling at her with insufferable good humor. Cat doubted that Mr. Hazelforth had ever met with any emotion or situation sufficiently unnerving to ruffle that smooth demeanor. It was galling that someone as provoking as he should look so collected. Rather than meet his cool blue gaze, Cat obstinately concentrated on the periphery of the scene and, by the time she reached the altar, felt not only ruffled, but rather cross-eyed as well. It was with no small amount of difficulty that she regained her equanimity and could turn to watch Uncle Martin hand Cecily to John as the ceremony began.

As Cat watched the bridal pair take each other's hands and repeat their vows, however, she felt her temper unbend a little. John and Cecily's love shone from their faces in a clear radiance. Cat's eyes grew uncharacteristically moist and she felt an aching catch in her throat. Would she ever know such happiness in the solitary life she had chosen for herself? Or, she wondered with a sniff of sheer self-pity, would the loneliness of the days to come overwhelm her and turn her into nothing but a disagreeable, lonely recluse?

Just then, she looked across the aisle to see Hazelforth smiling quizzically at her, as if daring her to call forth the wedding tears traditionally expected from her sex. Cat was determined to avoid them. She could not, would not, show any sign of female weakness to this loathsome man. Stubbornly, she pulled in her lower lip before it began to tremble. Then, her fingers sought out a thorn amid the roses she carried. Perhaps, she decided stoically, a little pain would allow her to master her unruly emotions. She bit her cheeks and stared straight ahead as the sharp pang stole focus. Impassively, she stood through the rest of the ceremony, almost oblivious to its content.

Before she knew it, Parson Tweedle had pronounced the couple man and wife, and Cat was suddenly forced to take Mr. Hazelforth's proffered arm and follow the happy couple out of the church. She stole a quick glance from beneath her heavy eyelashes, only to see him smiling at her with every appearance of good-natured innocence; only a slight crinkling at the corners of his very blue eyes, however, betrayed what she suspected to be a hint of mischief. She returned his smile coldly.

Looking more closely now, Cat could see that he appeared to be a somewhat older man than John, perhaps even thirty, for there was the beginning of silver in his curling blond hair. He was actually quite good-looking, although rather old, she reminded herself. Nevertheless, she found herself unaccountably wishing that she had held her tongue in the sacristy and not ruined herself in his estimation so quickly. As they reached the church steps, he leaned over solicitously to protect her from stray grains of rice which some village children were throwing with reckless enthusiasm, and Cat felt an unaccountable thrill race through her at his nearness. The pleasant scent of bay rum mixed with the fragrance of her own lavender in a heady swirl, as Hazelforth guided her through the crowds of well-wishers to a waiting phaeton which would follow the bride and groom back to Sparrowell. As he handed her in, she noticed to her chagrin that her wounded finger had left a spot of blood on the dove-gray of his sleeve. At her sharp intake of breath, his eyes followed hers to the offending stain.

"Miss Mansard, are you hurt?"

"I seem to have pricked my finger on my bouquet," she stammered in confusion, the color rushing to her cheeks. "I'm so sorry."

"No matter, my dear," he smiled at her, "but I should have thought that, as a rose with some thorns of your own, you'd be well aware of the hazards of seemingly innocent bouquets. I never trust roses myself."

"Nor should you," Cat countered, bristling at him once again. He might at least have expressed some sympathy for her poor finger which was now throbbing quite painfully. "Nor a Cat with its claws in velvet."

"Touché," Hazelforth returned with a tip of his hat.

Cat, and indeed the entire household, had their hands full during the reception. On the surface, all went smoothly, for guests were greeted, introductions made and nuptials toasted with apparent ease. However, the day was punctuated by the minor crises of the kitchen and cellar which always arise just when one is sure that plans for the entertainment have been perfected. While a fluttering Aunt Leah made sure that John's family and other important guests were properly attended to, Uncle Martin saw to the butler's concerns, and Cat found herself summoned several times for short conferences with Cook.

Even though her little dogs were spending the day sequestered out of harm's way in her chamber, the pair had been accused of somehow making off with a tray of miniature cream pastries. In spite of any and all precautions, Brutus and Caesar were often able to make their presence felt in the kitchen and were frequently, therefore, suspected when any culinary misfortunes arose. Their honor, however, had been cleared after a brief search of the auxiliary pantry, but Cook predicted in dark tones that some evidence of their skullduggery would surface before the day was much older. This worthy had generaled a long-term battle against the two dogs, and only the inducement provided by generous bonuses (which coincided, of course, with the dogs' forays into her realm) convinced her to remain at Sparrowell. Cat breathed a sigh of relief as she looked up to her chamber window and saw their noses pressed against it. She realized with customary resignation that they once again trespassed, boldly climbing up on her favorite love seat in order to watch the festivities below.

The day had grown quite warm, and the intensity of the brilliant sunshine had forced the ladies to unfurl their parasols. Cat only wished that she might avail herself of her fan as well, but the necessity of shaking hands with all and sundry as they passed through the receiving line precluded this relief. The number of well-wishers and the length of their effusions had kept Cat from further conversation with Mr. Hazelforth who stood at her side throughout the proceedings. For this reprieve she was glad. Her brief encounters with him thus far had left her feeling foolish, bad-tempered, and terribly, terribly young.

Cat had heretofore found herself the decided mistress of verbal sparring, but was forced to allow that she had not met anyone who had proved a real challenge until now. She was not at all sure she liked the notion of an equal match. She reflected with some dismay that her experience was not broad and her estimation of her own prowess in such matters had undoubtedly been inflated. It was easy enough to come off the victor in contests with Cecily and others of her small circle, and indeed those foppish fellows in Bath, but this older man of the world was quite another matter. One withering glance from those blue eyes, however good-humoredly they now sparkled when she encountered his glance, would doubtless defeat her without his having to so much as rouse himself to a defense. Above all things, Cat could not bear to look ridiculous, and so long as she felt their score had been left even, she determined to have as little further contact with the gentleman as was possible.

Early on in the reception, however, Cat caught the disagreeable sight of Snagworth collaring two young boys in the rose garden and disappearing with them into the house in an apparent fit of rage. All she needed was another emergency! At her groan of irritation, Mr. Hazelforth cast his eye in that direction as well. Looking about to ascertain whether the disturbance had been more generally noted, Cat quietly disengaged herself from the receiving line with as much grace as she could summon and made her way to the Hall with Hazelforth—uninvited, she fumed inwardly—following close upon her heels.

Just inside, they were met with the sight of a furious Snagworth shaking a pair of round-eyed, trembling youths whose torn and dirty party clothes revealed that they had indeed been up to some sort of rascalry. Snagworth's jowly face was trembling with dark fury as he snarled, "If I ever again catch the two of you in that garden or any part of it, I'll cut your hands off and feed them to those villainous dogs . . ."

"Snagworth!" Cat interrupted, appalled at such a speech. "Control yourself! Unhand those boys this instant!"

"Ah, Miss Catherine, best let me deal with this pair. You'd not say that if you knew aught of their black knavery," he retorted grimly without releasing his grip on their collars.

"Snagworth! Do not vex me further!" Cat snapped, reaching forward and drawing the terrorized boys away from him. "This sort of function is tedious to the young, and it is only to be expected that they might seek out some mischief where there is no amusement. I am sure they were only playing."

"Playing, you say! Playing!" Snagworth continued to rage, his face growing even more livid. "They was not playing! They was digging! Digging and pulling at those rose vines with never a thought to nothing but their own devilish destructiveness!"

"Watch your tongue, sir!" interrupted Hazelforth for the first time, in a tone that froze Snagworth where he stood. "James and Herbert, isn't it? I'm afraid you will have to excuse my young cousins, Miss Mansard. They appear to be depending on their new status in your family to overstep their bounds somewhat. Well, what is it boys? What were you about?" he demanded sternly.

James and Herbert hung their heads shamefacedly. Cat knelt down to their level and lifted their chins to meet her gaze. "No one will punish you, boys. I think I can guess what you were up to. Has Cecily been telling you stories about Sparrowell Hall?"

The boys nodded in unison. Then James, the elder of the two, spoke up with apparent bravery, now that the threat of punishment had been withdrawn. "She told us some wondrous stories, but we'd like to hear some more! Herbert and I were awake half the night to think we'd be coming here today and could look for treasure!"

"You see," Snagworth cried out, pointing his trembling finger at the dirty pair. "If they'd had a spade who knows where it would've ended?"

"Enough!" Cat interjected, not wishing Hazelforth to assert himself again on her behalf. She was quite capable of handling her own staff. "I am sorry to disappoint you, boys, but I am afraid that's all a legend. Oh, a pirate or two may have sought refuge in the harbor over the last four hundred years or so, but Cecily and I searched long ago for signs of them and found nothing. I'll tell you what, though. If you get yourselves cleaned up and have your tea, I'll show you something special and secret in the library. Would you like that?"

"Very much, thank you." The boys looked at each other. "You're sure about the treasure?"

"Quite sure, unfortunately," she told them. The boys took their leave, glancing daggers over their shoulders at Snagworth.

Cat straightened herself to her full height and looked sternly at the manager who was still fuming. "Snagworth, I suggest you confine your temper. We shall have no more outbursts. I have guests to attend to now, but I shall speak to you about this matter tomorrow morning." With that she turned and withdrew to the garden once more, Hazelforth at her elbow. The receiving line had broken up by the time they returned, and Cat was now flustered to find herself strolling among the guests with the very man whose company she had determined to avoid. She had very nearly lost her temper with Snagworth and was gratified that, for once, she had maintained some control. She wondered, however, whether he would have backed down so quickly were it not for Hazelforth's presence.

"What peculiar behavior all the way around," he remarked when they at last sat down to their tea. "I'm afraid the boys' deportment today won't improve your opinion of our family, Miss Mansard. I recall your saying we were still under consideration."

"I sometimes speak before I think," Cat said quietly as her color rose. "I hope you will forgive my sharp tongue and bad manners."

"Mine were no better, you will own, Miss Mansard. I fear that in society we often think too much before we speak—or laugh. One never knows for sure what's intended or what another person really thinks. I confess that your remark quite took me by surprise this morning, but I shouldn't mind being surprised more often. Forgive me my remark about the roses."

"There is nothing to forgive, for now we are even, I daresay. Shall we shake hands?" she asked smiling. He took her hand in his, and had she been more schooled in the ways of society, she would have known that he held it somewhat longer than was absolutely necessary. Suddenly agitated, she withdrew her hand and looked away as she attempted to regain her composure.

Changing the subject, she went on, "I find your young cousins charming. I hope they're not too disappointed—all I have to show them is the usual priest's hole and the secret passage. After a day of controlled decorum, it's refreshing to see two dirty-faced boys in hot pursuit of a dream."

"And your Snagworth in hot pursuit of them? You certainly put him to rout, though. I confess I'd no idea a lady could be so formidable!"

"I hope you are not laughing at me, Mr. Hazelforth. I had every reason to take the man to task!" Cat was mystified. She had not, after all, actually hit the wretched man with her parasol as she had envisioned doing when first she had beheld his bullying.

"Of course, you were entirely justified, Miss Mansard. I was not laughing at you, rather with you, I hope. But, really, have you ever seen yourself glower? The most alarming thing I ever saw! Why, you were even holding your parasol like a blunderbuss! I shall be surprised if the poor chap doesn't hand in his notice before the day's out."

"I will not have this, Mr. Hazelforth!" Cat exclaimed, frowning all the more. Although she loved to tease and torment others, one of her many faults was the inability to bear any baiting herself.

"There it is now!" Hazelforth went on recklessly, his blue eyes sparkling with an amusement

35

which Cat did not at all share. "That same glower. If I only had a glass for you to look into, Miss Mansard, you would be quite impressed with yourself! Most intimidating!"

"Why, Cat, whatever is the matter!" In some consternation Cecily had run up to join them. By now she had changed into her traveling costume and Cat was amazed to realize how much time must have passed.

"I am afraid your cousin has had her fill of my company for one day, my dear Cecily," Hazelforth told her with a laugh, as he bowed and retreated into the assembled crowd.

"How on earth did John ever come to be related to such an offensive man?" Cat fumed as she tucked her parasol discreetly under her arm. "I thought he had better taste!"

"Oh dear, Cat!" her cousin pouted. "I had such high hopes you two would take to each other. You have so much in common!"

"In common, Cecily! That man and I? What on earth can you be thinking of? Let me warn you, if you have had any of your marriage schemes in mind for us, you've quite outdone yourself in foolishness."

"Oh no, Cat! Marriage is quite the furthest thing I had in mind," Cecily said as she took her cousin's arm. "Why, Charles is every bit as committed to remaining single as you, for all he's just as good a catch. Society has quite despaired of him for that. Oh no! I would never dream of considering him for you."

"Well," Cat humphed, somewhat deflated. "Be sure that you don't."

"Now, John and I must be taking our leave in a few moments, for you know we plan to sail for the Continent tomorrow. I want to be sure that you come round front to watch me toss my bouquet." With that, Cecily ran to take John by the hand, looking well pleased with herself.

Well, that was fine, Cat thought to herself. Let Mr. Hazelforth make himself exclusive. That was certainly just fine with her. Quite refreshing, in fact. She could not for the life of her, however, determine why she should suddenly feel so dismal.

It seemed no time at all before there was a flurry in the crowd and the unmarried girls of the assembly hurried excitedly to the front of the Hall where John was already handing Cecily into his open coach. Just as Cat emerged from the front doorway, she heard Cecily call out her name. A half second later, she stood holding the bouquet which she had instinctively caught before she realized what it was. As the carriage pulled away, Cat found herself blushing self-consciously before the congratulations of the gathered well-wishers.

"Best wishes indeed, Miss Mansard," came the ironic voice of Mr. Hazelforth who had suddenly materialized at her side. "When may we wish you joy?"

"Save your breath, Mr. Hazelforth," Cat snapped, as she tossed the hapless bouquet high into the air with all the pent-up energy born of an extremely trying day. It landed, much to the crowd's delight, on a spire atop Sparrowell Hall.

Chapter Three

The days that followed the wedding were full with the business of setting things to order about the estate after the festivities, as well as helping Uncle Martin and Aunt Leah prepare for their remove to the Lake District. While time consuming and more than a little tedious, the activity kept Cat from missing Cecily too badly, and she had both the arrival of Miss Bartlett and her birthday to look forward to.

Cat's first order of business on the morning after the wedding was to dispatch one of the grounds keepers to remove Cecily's ill-fated bouquet from its perch atop the roof. She was soon forced to abandon this endeavor, however, when she was informed that a pair of larks had already set about establishing a nest in it. In spite of the blush it brought to her cheeks whenever she caught sight of it, Cat was softhearted with animals of all descriptions and she determined, therefore, that it must remain in its present location until the birds forsook it in the fall.

John's family had for the most part quitted the countryside for London immediately after the wedding, as the impending onset of the social season made it impractical to return to their homes before its commencement. Once or twice as Cat and the terriers set off on their morning walk, however, she had accidentally come upon Charles Hazelforth. He had delayed his departure for some days, using the opportunity, he said, to conclude some unfinished business in the area. Their encounters had been brief, but generally pleasant; moreover, since he displayed a rare fondness for her pets, spoiling and cosseting them every bit as much as she did, Cat found her exasperation in his presence lessening somewhat. During one of these encounters, Hazelforth had asked if he would be seeing her in London in the coming months.

"Cecily would have me there constantly," Cat replied, "for she fears my tendency to be reclusive and shun society. It is true, though, that I find more contentment in my library than in the drawing room."

"And yet you needn't confine yourself to those sorry quarters," Hazelforth reminded her. "I am surprised you do not go to the city if only to seek out the book shops. They are unsurpassed."

"The library at Sparrowell is adequate to my needs at present, but tell me—is that how you spend the entire Season? In bookstores?" Cat asked archly.

"Well, I must own that I do find myself at the occasional social gathering," he admitted, "but they needn't always be tedious or artificial, you know. I am afraid you have just had bad luck in the past. I go to London chiefly for the company, if you would know the truth. I have some particular friends there with whom I am sure even you would be delighted. And, as for the rest, they quite often make an interesting study. So you see, Miss Mansard, I share your feelings to some degree, but surely you cannot persuade me to believe you find amusement only in your books. Have you had no joy in the companionship of others?"

"Why yes, of course, but you see they must be most particularly in tune with my humors and sensibilities or we are almost at once at odds with one another. Indeed, I do find the country somewhat solitary, but that part of society which I observed lately in Bath would drive me to a *nunnery!*"

Here, Mr. Hazelforth quite gallantly bit back his amusement at her ignorance of this word's double entendre. He was altogether charmed, he realized, by her naïveté, particularly as it was clear she judged herself to be quite sophisticated. In fact, it was the first time in many years he had allowed a woman to charm him. It was also, he reminded himself, the first time he had met a woman whose mind was not inexorably bent on marriage. Yes, it was a refreshing change to feel as if he might be allowed to like a woman, develop a friendship with her, without fearing for his bachelorhood.

"I know I express myself too freely," Cat continued, "but tell me, Mr. Hazelforth, is there nowhere one can exercise one's wit and enjoy that of others without drawing censure? When I tried to talk of books in Bath, those fops looked me up and down with their infernal quizzing glasses as if I'd sprouted a second head!"

"Yes," Hazelforth agreed, laughing, "talk of books might well be thought outlandish by some of those poor louts. I wish I might have been there to witness their consternation. But, truly, was it merely talk of books that left them so dismayed?"

Cat looked down. "I fear I may have remarked upon their dress as well. But I am sure you would not blame me, Mr. Hazelforth, had you seen some of them decked out in such brocades and silks and intricate cravats, and such colors as defy good judgment! Peach and primrose and puce all in the same costume! I am quite sure I do not suffer from want of their company. No, if any wish my company, they must repair to the country, for I've no intention of forsaking it for some time!"

If truth be told, Cat had done more to become the topic of shocked conversation while in Bath than even she imagined. She not only disdained convention, but sometimes was altogether unaware that she had flouted it. She had appalled more than one family by inquiring closely into their business. Did they provide schools for the children of their estate workers? What did they do to ensure that the workhouses under their patronage were not guilty of the excesses of which she had heard? And what was to be done about the steadily growing number of orphans and homeless throughout the country?

Her aunt and uncle had remarked more than once in private that they felt Cecily's match was nothing short of miraculous, considering how often she was forced to go about in Catherine's company. They had grown to love their niece, in spite of the difficulties they had encountered in their years with her, but they were relieved that their responsibility toward her would soon be less. They would leave her to Miss Bartlett's care with all their good wishes, as well as a sigh of relief.

Miss Eveline Bartlett arrived on the evening before Cat's birthday and it was with delight she greeted this opportunity to once again be a part of Sparrowell Hall. It had been two years since Miss Bartlett had been at Sparrowell, being the last in a series of governesses who had one by one thrown up their hands in dismay at Cat's obstinate adherence to her unconventional ways.

During Miss Bartlett's brief tenure, she had seen both the heights and the depths of her career. In deportment, Cecily was all that she could ask for, while Cat drove her to distraction, questioning, deriding, and, finally, shrugging off the rules of propriety. Academically, the opposite was true, but for similar reasons. Where Cecily had been content to memorize submissively, Cat had constantly engaged Miss Bartlett in heated debates and the two of them often resorted to Sparrowell's well-stocked library to settle their disputes.

Miss Bartlett had been a good deal more successful in her dealings with Cat than any of her predecessors, and when she was called away to care for an ailing relation, she left her employ with a good deal of regret. Now that her role would be less repressive, she thought with good humor, she felt sure that she would enjoy her life. At first, the idea of chaperoning Catherine was daunting indeed, but knowledge of the girl's inclination for the quiet country life had stilled her fears.

The carriage conveying Miss Bartlett arrived just as the skies were beginning to darken, and Cat greeted her arrival with clear anticipation and enthusiasm. Although the weather had turned an ominous gray and the storm that had threatened all day had finally unleashed itself, Cat herself had run out with an umbrella and helped her new companion descend from the carriage.

"Let us get you upstairs at once," Cat cried, out of breath, as the pair twirled in the front door.

"Just a moment, let me see you, Catherine. Heavens, you've grown up, my dear!" Then she smiled with amusement in her warm brown eyes, "But are you really the young lady you seem?"

"Often, Miss Bartlett, but I fear not always," Cat admitted. "I am far better behaved than in the past, though, you may rest assured."

Cat ordered tea served in Miss Bartlett's chamber while Felicia unpacked for her. Soon they were cozily ensconced by a roaring fire, letting the rain fall if it would.

"What a grand time we shall have, Miss

Bartlett, for there are a dozen books of which I would talk with you! I am sorry you missed Cecily's wedding, but I must own it is good to have you all to myself."

"Yes, it is regrettable that I couldn't get away sooner, but I am sure I shall see Cecily when she returns from her wedding trip. There is one thing, Catherine," Miss Bartlett continued hesitantly. "Our relationship has changed somewhat now. Moreover, tomorrow you will be twenty. You may not know that I am but six and twenty. I know it is undoubtedly deepest vanity, but I feel as old as a church when you call me 'Miss Bartlett.' Do you think I could ask you to call me Eveline?"

Reaching to take her friend's hand, she replied with a smile, "If you will call me Cat!"

Cat arose early on the morning of her twentieth birthday and looked out over the hills, silver with dew. In the far distance, she could make out the soft haze rising from the gray sea. Storm clouds still hovered on the horizon, but it appeared that the day had a good chance of proving fair. On this auspicious day which marked the beginning of her adult responsibilities, she needed a good omen. Cat drew in a deep breath, shut her eyes, and firmly resolved that this year she would try to live up to the responsibilities of her new position, conduct herself with decorum and make Eveline happy that she had decided to return to Sparrowell. And, she thought wryly to herself, if I remain secluded in the country, I might very well adhere to my resolutions through the week.

Although there was to be no formal celebration, the day was nonetheless to be a full one. Cat would open her gifts after breakfast. Mr. Bagsmith, her solicitor, was expected sometime after that to go over the details of her coming of age. After luncheon, Aunt Leah and Uncle Martin planned to depart for the Lake District, and Cat intended to speak with Snagworth, not only about the estate, but also his odd outburst at the wedding reception. With one thing and another this item had been neglected; moreover, she felt a little ill at ease taking the man to task before Uncle Martin had officially handed the reins of power to her. But today she was determined that she would speak her mind.

Cat dressed carefully in a new white muslin gown which was embroidered minutely with violets and forget-me-nots. As it was early in the day, she let her dark curls hang loose and tied a violet velvet ribbon around them before she went downstairs. At the breakfast table she was greeted with good wishes from her aunt and uncle, as well as Eveline who had already joined them. Cat was delighted to see the first strawberries of the season and helped herself to the fresh cream that accompanied them. Uncle Martin arose and cleared his throat. "Before we begin, Catherine, I wish to propose a toast. Miss Bartlett, would we offend propriety if we began the day with some champagne?"

"I think not," she smiled mischievously, "although it seems most appropriate to be inappropriate on our Cat's birthday!"

Uncle Martin poured them each a tall sparkling glass. "To Catherine. May this day of new beginnings bring happiness to our Catherine and to all of us!"

After breakfast, Cat opened her packages. Eveline gave her a beautifully bound collection of Elizabethan poetry. Cecily and John had left antique amethyst earrings to match the drop Cat had worn the day of the wedding. From her aunt and uncle came an inlaid jewelry box which played a waltz when the lid was opened. Cat smiled at the significance of the tune: they had discussed a number of times the appropriateness of her learning this dance. "This was delivered this morning, as well," Uncle Martin said as he handed her a bouquet of new roses along with a card bearing Mr. Hazelforth's name. As Cat took the flowers, she noted with a rush of mixed feelings that the thorns had been carefully removed.

Soon after, the butler announced that Mr. Bagsmith had been shown to the library and was awaiting them there. As Aunt Leah and Uncle Martin arose to accompany her, Cat took Eveline's hand, "Please come along, too. For all my independence, I know I may be needing your advice before too long, so I will want you to be as familiar with my affairs as I am." The other woman, gratified at this confidence, rose with a smile, and the two entered the library arm in arm.

There they found a remarkable scene. An exasperated Mr. Bagsmith, who resembled nothing so much as newly boiled lobster, so red in face and bent over was he, was attempting to wrest a large envelope away from Brutus who had run behind the desk with it. As soon as Mr. Bagsmith's back was turned, Caesar helped himself to more papers from the solicitor's satchel. Aunt Leah and Uncle Martin began trying without much success to confine one or the other of the mischievous scamps, while Cat added her pleas to the general hubbub. If the truth were known, though, the naughty dogs paid as little attention to their mistress, who was notoriously lenient with them, as they did to anyone else. Finally after much coaxing and offering of treats, the two were finally captured and taken away, wagging their stubby tails, blithely ignoring any and all attempts to shame them.

"Ahem," Mr. Bagsmith began, much disgruntled, "I hope you will not mind the chewed corners, Miss Mansard. I can assure you that it will not affect their legality, although much of their aesthetic quality is now lost." Mr. Bagsmith prided himself on the excellent penmanship of his clerks and he stared down at the tattered documents dismally.

"I am very sorry for the trouble, Mr. Bagsmith," Cat began, although the smile she tried to hide belied this statement. "Do let us begin."

Mr. Bagsmith made a great show of arranging his various papers, but finally cleared his throat and looked up at Cat. "You know to some extent,

I believe, the terms of your grandmother's will. That is, you are her only heir and are to come into the estate upon reaching this, your twentieth birthday. There are, however, some rather unusual details which she wished to have kept from you until this day, Miss Mansard."

Cat's mind raced. What on earth could the will hold of which she was not already aware? Uncle Martin and Aunt Leah looked puzzled as well.

Mr. Bagsmith, basking in their attention, went on. "It was your grandmother's desire that if you had reached your twentieth birthday without having wed, *other* conditions to your inheriting would come into effect. These are outlined both in a codicil and in this letter which she wished you to read in the event you were still unmarried." Here he paused and handed Cat a sealed letter.

Cat sat stunned, holding the letter in her hands for several moments. Then she slowly opened it, tears starting in her eyes at the sight of the familiar slanting handwriting:

My dearest Cat,

What your thoughts are today I cannot tell, but I can assure you with all my love that what I do is for your benefit. I have often pondered whether I did right to let you grow up so independent in thought and action, for though I know this suits your nature best, I have feared you will incur the censure of society. Also, it is clear that you may be overly content with your own com-

49

pany to the extent that you will not seek out acquaintanceships that will lead to marriage. I know your general opinion of the world, my dear, but let me assure you that somewhere exists a partner who will cherish you for your true worth and one whom you can cherish in return.

Lest you miss this best part of life, I have laid down some strictures which I hope you will not resent too much (though I can picture with some apprehension what your first reaction will be):

First, as you are not likely to find a mate in the library at Sparrowell Hall, you will spend the Season each year in London until you are married. Yes, even until you are old and gray, although I doubt very much it will come to that.

Second, as I know your nature as well as anyone, I require that you offer proofs to my solicitor on a regular basis that you are indeed taking part in the doings of society by attending such balls, routs and other invitations as come your way.

Third, should you fail in regard to either of these requirements, you will be enjoined to marry whomsoever is deemed most fit by my solicitor or forfeit all claim on your inheritance, but for £1,500 per annum.

Believe me, Catherine, that I know best and, however heartless I must now seem, wish only for your happiness. I have lived

long, known both love and loneliness, and
pray that you will find the former.
                    All my love,
                    Alice Mansard

The others had watched with curiosity turning
to concern, as Cat's expression changed from interest to petulance to shock. Once she was finished reading she rose and walked deliberately
from the room without saying a word or respond-
ing in any way to their questioning looks.

From the library Cat proceeded directly to the
grounds and soon lost herself among the paths as
she wildly surveyed her new and disagreeable condition. Cat had never before thought of her grandmother in angry terms, and found she could not,
even now, but railed inwardly against fate in general. She had so looked forward to the independence and liberty she had long assumed today
would bring her. Now she would be more firmly
controlled and faced with more serious consequences for untoward behavior than ever before.
How could Gran have done such a thing? The
very thought of spending her favorite time of year
in London was depressing, to say nothing of the
disagreeable company she would be forced to
keep. And how could she curb her behavior
enough to even be invited anyplace more than
once? Then Cat saw the shrewdness of her grandmother's strictures: she *must* school herself in propriety, learn to control herself, and quickly adopt
the manners preferred by society, or forfeit the

home she loved, for she must surely refuse to wed some stranger chosen by Mr. Bagsmith! The idea of marrying at all, when she had sworn many times, and often in public, that such a thing would never be, was humiliating! Surely her pride would never recover.

Cat was disheartened by more than just hurt pride and the surface conditions prescribed by the will, however. She had thought that, by making her the sole heir, Gran had trusted her. And yet, as Cat mentally reviewed her behavior over the last several years, even at Cecily's wedding, she could see that, to some degree, her grandmother's concern was well warranted. Without more discipline and at least an attempt to conform to society's strictures, the day must surely come when she would have offended most of her acquaintance. Though Cat enjoyed her solitude, she was not prepared to be entirely a recluse.

As Cat wandered, stunned and confused at the news the day had brought, the weather changed to reflect her inner turmoil. She had come to the edge of the land overlooking the rocky coast as the once blue sky began to cloud over and darken. The wind came up chillingly and a drenching rain began to fall. Soon Cat was wet through, her fine muslin dress clinging and hair curling damply about her face. Behind her came the sound of quick footsteps and she put her face in her hands. Poor Uncle Martin must have been forced into this foul weather to seek her out.

"Miss Mansard, come at once into this copse

and take some shelter!" Cat was shocked to hear Mr. Hazelforth's voice. What on earth must he think now to see her in such a state? She felt his hand take her arm and guide her to the nearby stand of trees. There, Cat realized to her deep chagrin that her wet gown now clung most revealingly to her form, and she quickly crossed her arms over her bosom in a futile attempt at modesty.

"Here, take my coat," Hazelforth offered and he draped it over her shoulders. Although it, too, was wet quite through, Cat took comfort in concealment, clutching the lapels of the deep blue superfine well up to her chin as she shuddered with wretched embarrassment. This was surely the worst day in a bad life! Then, when she turned to thank him, she was even more chagrined to encounter the sight of Hazelforth in his shirtsleeves and waistcoat. Through the dampened fabric she could clearly see the delineation of his well-muscled form and even an intimation of flesh-tones. She could only conjecture with dismay how much of her own rosiness might have been revealed through the even thinner muslin.

"Your family and Miss Bartlett are concerned, Miss Catherine," he broke in after a moment. "They were just setting out to find you when I came by to take my leave of you. Here, wipe your face on my handkerchief." Cat did so, sniffing back her tears with an unseemly gulp. If he were to begin teasing her now, she reflected darkly, she was quite sure she would do him some bodily harm. Fortunately, however, Hazelforth stood silently by and restrained himself from making any comment or inquiry while she struggled to regain her composure as best she could.

As Hazelforth stood watching Cat trying desperately to recover herself, teasing her was the farthest thing from his mind. As the trees above dripped down on her pitiful form, it was all he could do to resist the urge to take her into his arms and comfort her like a small child. He found this impulse altogether mystifying. He usually regarded the emotional excesses of the opposite sex with disdain or, at best, bewildered amusement — never with such commiseration as he was now experiencing.

He did not know what exactly it was that had upset her, but from the looks on the faces of her family, he was sure it must be a matter of some enormity. As she struggled to contain her tears, he could not help but admire her. In spite of her wet nose and glistening eyes, he thought she looked altogether charming — although he was fairly certain that would not be her own assessment of her appearance. Moreover, he was equally aware that a girl of her spirit and pride must be chagrined for him to have discovered that there was a soft, vulnerable side to her prickly nature.

"The rain has let up a little," he finally said. "We must take advantage of it and get you indoors again before you take a chill."

As they made their silent way down the path, the clouds did begin to part a little and some warmth returned. Just before they were within view of the Hall, Hazelforth paused. "You offered me your hand in friendship, I believe, some days past. I do not know the nature of your concerns, Miss Mansard, but if you ever have need, be assured that you may depend on that friendship. I will be leaving the district tomorrow morning, but I will call before I depart, if I may, to assure myself that no harm has come of this wetting."

Cat finally turned to smile wryly up at him, "It is no great problem, Mr. Hazelforth. My headstrong response to having my way thwarted is, like King Lear, to cast myself into the throes of a tempest. But I thank you for your concern and civility—and your restraint. I know I must make a tempting target for some jest or another."

"Indeed, Miss Catherine, you misjudge me," he said in a low voice, for they had now reached the door. "I would not distress you now for all the world."

Before Cat could further reply, she was gathered in by Felicia who had been keeping watch, and rushed upstairs. The maid, a great respecter of her mistress's moods, asked no questions, but wrapped her up in quilts and set her in front of the fire. The rains resumed, and Cat took what comfort she could from tea and toast, avoiding as best she could an analysis of her overwrought emotions. None of them, she concluded, bore close scrutiny.

Some short time had passed when Eveline tapped lightly at the door and entered Cat's chamber smiling mildly. "It seems our situation here will not be what we expected, Cat. Mr. Bagsmith took the liberty of informing us of the conditions governing your inheritance. I am sorry this will be so difficult for you."

"And for you as well, Eveline, for this involves you as closely as me. I know you envisioned a quiet life at Sparrowell, and it is clear that the future can offer you nothing but annoyance from me." Cat paused to wipe another self-pitying tear from her cheek. Then she took a deep breath, "I am prepared to release you from your commitment, if you wish, Eveline."

"I wouldn't desert you now, Cat, although I admit I find these strictures somewhat trying myself. Nevertheless, there it is. What can we do about it?"

Cat shrugged. "Very little it seems. I suppose we must take what time we have to prepare for this trial, for I can see no hope but to become one of the mob of husband seekers. I can face many things in life, but the loss of my dear Sparrowell is not among them. Tomorrow, perhaps, you will start by drilling me in deportment again, distressing as I am sure we both find that endeavor. But I assure you, I shall strive to be a far more attentive pupil than I was some years ago."

"We shall begin with the question of whether it is seemly to have a man's coat draped across your bed!" Eveline observed as she held up the damp and rumpled garment. "It was most kind of Mr. Hazelforth to fetch you in. Your uncle would have gone, but he's of an age where he must avoid risking his health and we could not send a servant for fear of gossip when you can least afford it. Tell me, Cat. Mr. Hazelforth has paid you some marked attention of late, I understand. He seems an agreeable sort. Could it be that he would make an offer for you and solve your problems quickly?"

Cat looked down abashed. "We are friends, Eveline, that is all. Moreover, he has on more than one occasion had the misfortune to see me at my worst. In any case, Cecily has informed me he is a confirmed bachelor."

Eveline shrugged resignedly. "I suppose you know best, Cat, if his attentions are mere friendship. Now, if you are feeling somewhat recovered, your aunt and uncle are concerned. They are debating whether they should postpone their journey and stay here with you a while."

"Oh dear! I have been terribly selfish, haven't I? I had best get dressed and reassure them. They've spent enough of their lives on my business and I know they are anxious to return home."

Cat turned quickly to repairing her toilette, her good humor returning somewhat, for while her emotions were volatile, it was one of the great strengths of Cat's personality that she could not remain angry or distressed for long. Already, she was thinking ahead to London.

Chapter Four

Cat awakened late the next day weighed down by the heavy feather comforter Felicia had piled on her as a precaution against taking a chill. Caesar and Brutus had climbed up during the night and were burrowed deeply into the feather cover, their little black noses resting boldly on Cat's eyelet pillow cases. "I'm not the only one around here in need of discipline," she yawned, prodding the protesting pair noisily onto the floor. She then rang for Felicia, who soon appeared bearing a tray of steaming tea, scones, and marmalade.

"You'd best stay snug in bed today, Miss Cat. It's wretched gray weather anyway, pouring down tubs and buckets it is, and I won't have you racing about and taking ill. Out of my way, you corrupt black-guards!" Felicia muttered darkly, kicking as best she could at the bouncing terriers without upsetting her tray. "These scapegrace beasts will cause no end of trouble in London, mark my word, for I've not the least doubt you plan to take them with you."

"So," Cat sighed resignedly, "you already know I plan to go to London, do you?"

"Well, Miss Cat," Felicia shrugged as she finally set down her tray, "we servants can't help having ears, you know, for all the gentry treats us like we're deaf and dumb. Your aunt was that upset yesterday, keening and wailing that she'd never see her home again. It was right of you to send them along their way, no doubt about it."

"I am glad of your approval, Felicia," Cat sniffed. "Pray what else of my affairs do you know?"

"Only that this is not your doing," the maid continued, unabashed. "We talked it up and down in the servants' hall over tea last evening and we all decided it must have something to do with that Mr. Bagsmith's visit yesterday, for things was nice as ever you please when, all the sudden, out into the storm you run, up starts the wailing, and now we're off to London when you said you'd never." Felicia paused for a breath long enough to take two biscuits from her apron pocket and toss them out the door to the hallway. Then she speedily closed the door behind Caesar and Brutus who were after the unexpected treats like a shot.

"Now maybe you can have your breakfast in peace," the maid continued. "Anyway, I starts thinking to myself, the only reason for a young lady to go off to London this time of year is to find a husband. I wouldn't breathe a word of this to them other vile gossips, you may well trust, but tell me if I'm not right."

"Unfortunately, you are, Felicia. I just hope word of this won't get around, or I'll be the subject of a scandal before I even have a chance to try to conduct myself with proper decorum." Cat bit grumpily into a scone.

"Decorum!" Felicia snorted in scornful disbelief. "When was you ever concerned with decorum?"

So it was that Cat found herself confiding the effect of her grandmother's letter to Felicia, who listened, eyes wide and jaw agape with rapt attention.

"Oh, Miss Cat, was there ever anything so exciting? Just like in the penny novels I get from Cook! The lady of beauty and fortune compelled to marry against her wishes! Oh, my dear heart!"

"I sincerely wish it were a novel, Felicia, for it is going to put a crimp in my style and no mistake. Do you realize what it means to be constrained by decorum? You and I could never have this manner of conversation, except that we do so on the sly. Ladies of *decorum* do not converse with their maids so freely. I must act mild, demure, cast down my eyes, defer to elders, simper about men, and, worst of all, cut cold those people who act as I so often do. It's beastly, Felicia. But there's no avoiding it, so I'd best be up and about. I review my deportment lessons starting today."

"Oh, Miss Cat! I almost forgot. That Mr. Hazelforth was by already, but had to be off in good time this morning, he told Chumley. Said he just called to pay his compliments and inquire after your health, he said."

"How long ago was this?"

"Oh, an hour and more."

"What on earth is the time?" Cat cried, leaping from her bed and heading for her vanity table.

"After eleven, I should think. You did sleep well and I thought it best to let you be."

Cat felt her spirits dampen unreasonably on hearing that she had missed her morning visitor. Mr. Hazelforth had proved to be far more agreeable than she had originally anticipated, and she was beginning to value his friendship a good deal more than she would ever have thought possible. She had not realized how starved she was for intelligent conversation. That must surely be the reason her heart fluttered a little when she saw him, she told herself. Besides, he had been so kind and understanding and circumspect yesterday. Her emotions were too ruffled just now to bear closer examination, but she did wish she had been able to thank him for his kindness. That was all, wasn't it?

Completing her toilette with amazing rapidity, Cat proceeded to the drawing room where she found Eveline already busily drawing up a plan of study.

"You will be glad to find, Cat dear, that our chore will not prove so taxing as you feared. Your dancing was always quite good, I recall. Your manners at table, as well, as long as you remember to have a good meal before you leave the house so you can pick daintily at your food in public. I am a little afraid your healthy appetite wouldn't bear close examination."

"Well, I'll have a chop or two and a tart in my chamber before dinner. That should do the trick," Cat pronounced. "Go on now, Eveline. I know the worst is coming."

"It's your conversation, I'm afraid, that requires the most attention," Eveline told her with a rueful glance. "I believe you know the rules as well as any. You have merely determined to flout them and it's become automatic now. What I propose is that we concoct some sort of practice — exercises, if you will. I shall compose a list of hypothetical situations for us to work from. Then I shall play a role and you will respond to me. Together, I believe we can contrive a host of polite scripts. What say you, Cat?"

"I suppose it cannot hurt," Cat mused. "You are quite correct about my conversation. I do find that the most shocking comments rise to my lips almost of their own accord. Perhaps practice would be the very thing for me. Indeed, you make it sound almost diverting, Eveline — like playacting."

"Well, so it is. You remember Shakespeare said, 'I hold the world but as the world, Gratiano. A stage where every man must play his part . . .' "

" '. . . and mine a sad one,' " Cat finished the quote in dramatic tones. "When shall we begin?"

"As soon as I have made up a list of possible scenarios. In the meantime, I think that you might spend your time considering some of the particulars of this adventure. You must contact Mr. Bagsmith about letting an appropriate house in London and engaging a staff. I suspect that he will already have begun that endeavor. I'm also afraid that you will need someone to act as your sponsor in London. I can serve adequately as companion and chaperon, but I cannot hope to introduce you to society and contrive invitations for you. What you need is an established member of the *ton*. Can you think of any relative or acquaintance in London who could serve in that role?"

"No relation, of that I am sure," Cat reflected. "Uncle Martin is no help—he has always been a simple country squire and is just released from duty as it is. I have no other blood relations."

"What of Cecily's new family? Surely they would be happy to see to you. And you are such good friends with Hazelforth . . ."

"Heavens, no!" Cat responded with such sudden vehemence that Eveline was forced to look quite narrowly at her. "John's family wouldn't do at all—I can hardly claim any intimacy there. Besides, Cecily and John are away on their wedding trip and they will be gone for some time yet. I really could not bring myself to broach this subject without them."

"I suppose you're right, Cat," Eveline agreed disconsolately. "Well, I must say, you are in a quandary indeed."

"Whatever am I to do then, Eveline? It must be someone I know. Some details of this wretched situation must be communicated to whomever does agree to sponsor me, yet I don't wish to introduce such a delicate subject or relate such intimate details to near strangers. Let me think a moment," Cat continued as she paced back and forth about the room. "There is Lady Montrose, my godmother, but I have heard very little from her in recent years. She was a close friend of my grandmother—heavens! She must be at least as old as Methuselah by now! I wonder, though, if she would be up to such an undertaking?"

"That sounds like the very thing. I suggest you write to her today, Cat. You needn't reveal all of your situation until you meet her and decide how much is necessary or advisable. Now, I will begin working on the conversation exercises, while you attend to the details of your business."

As Cat made her way to the library, she thought how fortunate she was to have Eveline. Once it was clear that there was no way of circumventing her grandmother's wishes, Cat could see little value in wailing, whining or lamenting the situation. The most intelligent thing for her to do was to carry on and be about the necessary business to achieve the most desirable end to this dilemma. In this endeavor, Eveline's calm demeanor and competent approach were more heartening to Cat than any amount of sympathy or fussing would have been.

For most of the morning, Cat was up to her elbows in papers and correspondence. She hoped that Mr. Bagsmith would be able to find a suitable house in an acceptably fashionable neighborhood. She had decided that she would take some members of the Sparrowell staff to the city with her. It would be diverting for them and comforting for her to be surrounded by familiar faces. She knew that Felicia, for one, would look forward to the interlude away from the country, and was convinced that few others could take her place.

Having made several lists of things which must be attended to in the weeks before her remove to London, Cat now turned her efforts to her letter to Lady Montrose. Cat had dutifully written to her each year, but had received responses somewhat erratically, particularly in later years. There had been an occasional gift from her godmother from time to time, but these were apparently sent according to whim, for their arrival never coincided with either Christmas or Cat's birthday. Also, these gifts ranged from the sublime to the decidedly ridiculous. Once there had been a pair of ruby-encrusted combs; another time an elephant foot umbrella stand; still another time a caricaturist's version of Lady Montrose and Cat's grandmother as young ladies.

There had never been any question that Lady Montrose was very high *ton* indeed; it was, however, unclear whether her sponsorship would confer on Cat the sort of conventional aura that she now required. There was no one else, however, so Cat set about composing her letter. This task took some time, for the wording was difficult; it was necessary, Cat felt, to be clear as to the particulars of her visit, but subtle as to its importance and purpose — at least until Cat was able to meet the lady in person and make an assessment of her circumspection. There was also the problem of Lady Montrose's age and very likely diminished memory. Would she remember immediately who Cat was and why she felt she could draw on her sponsorship?

When Cat had finished that task with some degree of satisfaction, she rang for a servant to take her letters to the post and to summon Snagworth to her. She faced this last problem with some consternation. She did not feel entirely secure leaving Sparrowell Hall under Snagworth's sole administration for such a long duration, but there certainly was not enough time to engage a new manager and familiarize him with the property in the short time that remained.

Snagworth's behavior had certainly posed a puzzle lately. Cat had mentioned her concerns briefly to Uncle Martin, but he had seemed untroubled by them. She could not help feeling a little foolish, after all, for what had the man actually done? Chastised some overly bold children and behaved oddly in the walled garden. There was some justification for his conduct with the boys, although the ferocity of his admonitions certainly went too far. Perhaps, Cat told herself, the real reason for her discomfiture with him was wounded pride on her part. He really did not treat her as if she were the mistress of the Hall. Perhaps he was right, she reflected dismally. Whether she would actually hold that title was in some doubt now.

Cat did, however, attempt to look as daunting as possible when Snagworth was announced. She fixed him with a dark stare as he came smiling and bowing into the room, rubbing his hands together in an unpleasantly servile manner.

"Ah, Miss Catherine, so you're off to the pleasures of London so soon. Well, well, well. We can't hardly blame you for looking for a little excitement, a little diversion. You just go along to your fancy balls and operys and stay as long as ever you please, my dear, and don't worry your head a bit about auld Sparrowell Hall. Auld Snagworth's here, yes, indeed."

Snagworth's manner and apparent anxiousness to see her gone did nothing to relieve Cat's apprehension. She took a deep breath.

"Snagworth," she began, "I do not know how long I shall be away, but I have requested that Mr.

Bagsmith look in on the estate from time to time during my absence. I myself may return at any time, so I would like the Hall to be held in readiness. I shall leave a number of the staff here for that purpose."

Cat hoped that an understanding of Mr. Bagsmith's proposed visits and the veiled threat of her own imminent return would be enough to convince Snagworth her absence would not constitute an opportunity for mischief. She wasn't quite sure what she suspected him of, but she always trusted her intuition. Snagworth, however, seemed unbothered by this little speech.

"Yes, Miss Catherine, yes indeed. You'll find everything right as rain, just as your uncle would have it. No need to worry on that account . . ."

"Snagworth," she interrupted sharply, "I am the mistress of the estate. My uncle is gone now. The estate will be run as *I* would have it, and I will thank you very much to remember it."

"Is that right, Miss Catherine?" Snagworth smiled at her innocently. "And just what is it you would propose to change?"

"Your manner to begin with!" she cried indignantly. Then mastering herself once more, she went on, "I am forced to be gone sooner than I had planned, but we shall discuss this matter in detail another day. If any problems arise, you will inform Mr. Bagsmith immediately. Also, I am going to ask that you attempt to curb your temper. I do not want a repeat of the scene I witnessed at Miss Cecily's wedding reception, regardless of what offense you perceive is being committed."

Snagworth bowed his head and sighed in a much afflicted tone. "Well, Miss Catherine, I was only doing my duty to you, protecting your property like, but there's some efforts that's just not to be appreciated. No, indeed. If they come after your walls with sledgehammers, why next time, I'll invite them to sit down to tea. I don't like to give offense, not at all."

"There's no need to be facetious, Snagworth. I think we understand each other quite well. That will be all," Cat dismissed him in an even tone. As Snagworth backed out of the room, bowing and smiling all the while, Cat felt a chill go up her spine. She had the feeling that something was very wrong, but what? Once again, Snagworth had done nothing she could pinpoint to justify her anxiety. She hoped with all her heart that she was mistaken.

Chapter Five

Between Eveline's surprisingly entertaining deportment lessons and taking care of details for their stay in London, the days that followed passed quickly. Each morning began with Cat and Eveline's practicing a different dialogue: table talk with a tedious dinner partner; polite chitchat with a nosy matron who could not be offended; managing importunate rakes on and off the dance floor. These lessons soon became Cat's favorite portion of the day, for, as often as not, the two women found themselves overcome by the hilarity of their fictional situations. Cat found herself greatly diverted in Eveline's company, particularly when she contrasted the latter's current lightheartedness with the solemnity with which she had conducted the schoolroom only a few years earlier.

"What a time you must have had to maintain your composure with Cecily and me," Cat exclaimed one day during their exercises.

"Indeed," Eveline replied with a laugh, "it would

have done my classroom's discipline little good had the two of you realized how often I was forced to retreat to my chamber convulsed in laughter. How liberating it is to at last acknowledge that life is a very amusing endeavor!"

"You mean you were not departing in a fury?" Cat exclaimed.

"Quite the opposite, I assure you," Eveline laughed, her brown eyes now sparkling merrily. "Do you recall the time you dipped the kitten's paws in the inkwell so you could trace its movements?"

"Well, if it had not chosen to walk across my Latin conjugations I doubt you would ever have known!"

"Very likely not, except for the fact that it also made its way up the skirt of Cecily's new lawn dress without her knowing. She was always so particular about her appearance that the sight was doubly amusing"

"It's a little embarrassing to own that I was up to such tricks at the age of sixteen!"

"I shouldn't be a bit surprised if you were to try it again tomorrow," Eveline laughed. "Oh dear! Do you think we need add some polite explanations to your repertoire to account for such doings?"

"Very likely," Cat admitted, only a little facetiously.

For the most part, though, their lessons were more than merely diverting, and, as a result, Cat was ultimately in possession of a variety of courteous evasions and the mistress of polite prattle. These verbal formulas would do very nicely, she felt sure, to guarantee her entrance to, and continued acceptance in, society.

70

Cat was determined, of course, to act and speak with greater honesty to those men whose romantic interest she engaged. It would be fair to no one to present an entirely false front, nor could she consider marriage to anyone who did not know her true personality. She felt certain that there must be someone who, beneath the false front enforced by society, shared her tastes and views. If she had to continue her visits to London for the next two or three years to find him, then so be it. It was not a terribly palatable prospect, she sniffed to herself, but there seemed to be little way around it.

Cat was too stubborn to admit even to herself that the excitement she felt rising daily was the result of anticipation rather than a case of nerves. Neither would Cat have been pleased were it generally known how often her thoughts were occupied by one Charles Hazelforth. She had imagined that as time went on her encounters with him would fade from her memory. On the contrary, each seemed to be etched indelibly: every word of every conversation, every intonation. Indeed, Cat had been caught off-guard on a number of occasions when Eveline or Felicia remarked on the deep blushes that rose to her cheeks when she suddenly found herself reliving the more embarrassing moments.

Cat was content to let observers imagine that it was mere consternation at her enforced participation in the London Season which occasioned her agitation; however, it was with a great deal of perplexity that she more and more often caught herself envisioning meetings with Hazelforth in and about London.

All too often, the image of him walking toward her, his face suffusing with a smile as it so often had during the days after Cecily's wedding rose up before her. She had found herself looking forward to those accidental meetings during her morning walk. She wondered, too, if he had found them as gratifying as she, and if indeed their encounters had been as coincidental as they seemed. But this was foolishness, she told herself sternly. What on earth, she wondered, was responsible for such idle fantasies? It was altogether likely that she would never even see that gentleman in town.

Mr. Bagsmith's search for a suitable house was short-lived, for when Lady Montrose's reply arrived, it was soon clear that she would hear of no such thing. Cat and Eveline were to stay at Montrose House, and there would be no further discussion. Lady Montrose had kept a reduced household in recent years, but since she expected to do some entertaining during Cat's stay, she would welcome any of Cat's staff she wished to bring. This solved one of Cat's problems more easily than she had imagined, and she hoped sincerely that she and her godmother would suit. She was much comforted by the fact that Lady Montrose had been her grandmother's bosom friend in their girlhood, and she found herself looking forward to this aspect of her adventure with a good deal of anticipation.

Cat packed very little beyond what she would need for her journey, for, upon their arrival, an errand of primary importance would be a visit to the modiste. What passed for fashion in the provincial environs of Sparrowell Hall would never do for London society, which seemed to change its criteria for hats, sleeves, and waistlines with the phases of the moon. Something would have to be done with her companion's wardrobe as well, for surely Lady Montrose's advanced age would necessitate the role of chaperon falling to Eveline more often than not. That sensible creature, too, it seemed would be forced to be a slave to the whims of style.

As the weeks went by, Brutus and Caesar fell victim to an energetic nervous excitement as they watched their mistress's preparations go forth. They ran up and down stairs, were accidentally shut up in cupboards, barked for sheer pleasure, and generally made themselves even more annoying than ever. Cook, though, was in a good mood for once, for she was off to visit her sisters in Cornwall for the duration of Cat's absence. Since Lady Montrose employed the services of a French chef, it was generally concluded that the volatile territory of the kitchen could suffer but one ruler.

Cat's butler, Chumley, would stay on at the Hall. Although he was somewhat young for that position, his family had been part of Sparrowell's staff for more than a hundred years, and his own father had been butler before him. His presence would allay Cat's fears about Snagworth to some degree, and she was grateful that she could call upon him to do her this service, particularly since the prospect of spending time in London was in all probability quite as attractive to him as any other member of the staff. She promised herself that she would make it up to him in some way.

* * *

The day of their departure for the city dawned as fair and clear as any could hope for. The journey to London would take most of two days, barring accident, even in this fine weather. So it was that the sky was still changing from the pinkish lavender of sunrise to the unclouded azure of the day to come as the two heavily laden carriages pulled away from Sparrowell Hall.

The first party consisted of Cat, Eveline, and Felicia, packed in among an enormous number of pillows to cushion them against the bone-wrenching ride. Caesar and Brutus jumped blithely from lap to lap, and pressed their wet noses on the windows, clearly beside themselves with joy at the prospect of this rare outing. The second carriage held four servants: two parlor maids, a footman, and a boy of all work, in somewhat less comfort, but equal excitement.

The first several miles of their route were fairly familiar, and because the weather was so agreeable, the party was able to picnic along their route at midday, rather than trust their luck (and stomachs) to the dubious hospitality of inn fare. The servants spread blankets on the grass in a little glen and unpacked the baskets. Soon, they were all munching companionably on glazed pheasant, Stilton cheese, hothouse grapes, and herbed bread, glad of the warm sunshine and the stillness of the day. Martin, the boy of all work, tossed scraps to the two terriers, keeping them at bay while the others ate.

Watching these antics, Cat wondered how long it would be before she would again be able to spend time so enjoyably and with such ease. She had known these servants from childhood, had even played with some of them under her grandmother's lenient care. Tonight at the inn, the servants' quarters would be cramped and probably dirty, their fare less agreeable than hers, and such democratic behavior as at this idyllic picnic would be absolutely out of the question. She and Eveline would be housed upstairs and the servants very definitely downstairs, with the exception of Felica who would haunt the limbo in between. Cat was not at all content with this arrangement, but the inn at which they would stop tonight, The Ivy Tree, was situated prominently on the main road; word of any untoward deportment would undoubtedly cause talk, and word of it would rapidly spread through that remarkable grapevine — serving hall gossip.

As Cat and her party continued on their journey through the warm afternoon countryside, to pass the time, Eveline read aloud to those passengers in the first carriage, while in the second carriage, the servants excitedly exchanged tales they had heard of the various wonders of London life.

"I shouldn't wonder we'll see the Prince Regent himself while we're there," Betsy, one of the parlor maids, was saying in respectful tones. "I'd dearly love to have a look at a royal, I would."

"Well, that one would dearly love to have a look at you, my dear, and the closer the better," Tom, the footman, returned with a knowing smirk. "You'd turn the head of the Regent quick enough and no mistake."

"Well, I've heard that's no trick," Audrey, the second parlor maid, sniffed dismissively. "I've heard not even an aged grandmother's safe around *that* one, so I guess even our Betsy might do well to watch her backside. Unless, of course, she wants to see His Highness up close!"

"You're just a jealous cat," Betsy huffed, " 'cause you haven't got my looks. I'm sure I don't know what you'll do in London on your half-day, but if I'm in a very good mood I might let you keep watch for my followers."

"Oh, I know what I'll do in London and no mistake. But it's none of your business, so I'll thank you not to ask," Audrey sneered, her bad temper doing little for her unremarkable looks.

"Ho-hum, well I'm so interested, aren't I? Don't forget to let me know when you're ready to tell us all the details so I can be sure to take my nap. What'll you do in London, Tom?" Betsy asked, turning her smiling attention to the footman.

"Oh, I expect to see the sights," Tom replied with an air of great experience. "There's sights in London, I hear tell, that sets a man off the country for life."

"Oh, I'd like to know what!" exclaimed Martin. "This is an adventure I wouldn't miss, and London is sure to be a wonder, but I'll always go back to Sparrowell Hall. That's the life for me."

"You may well think that now," Tom went on in a jaded tone. "but we shall hear a different tune a few weeks hence."

Chapter Six

The remainder of their journey was not to be so uneventful as the first day had promised. The Ivy Tree had proved unremarkable except in the blandness of the food and the dinginess of the decor, and the remaining half day's ride from there to London should have passed quickly. The party had hardly been on the road half an hour, however, when the sound of galloping hoofbeats behind them intruded on the quiet of the morning.

As the horseman came alongside the first carriage, the sharp report of a musket's fire brought the horses to a frenzied halt and the sound of a muffled voice could be heard by the shocked passengers, "Stand and deliver or be drownded in a pool of blood!" Then the musket was fired into the air once again.

Cat peeked out the window of the carriage in an understandably cautious manner and took stock of the situation. "I'll just be a moment," she said to her white-faced companions. "You two stay right here."

Before they could protest, she hopped lightly from

the carriage onto the lane. Before her, on a horse whose sagging bones and lethargic eye bore witness to the end of a long career at the plow, sat a figure curiously draped, bundled, and masked, wearing an obviously false beard of an unlikely reddish hue.

"Your money or your life!" the man growled, pointing his musket at her.

"Indeed?" Cat returned coolly. "And how do you propose to convince me that I should part with either?"

"I would not hesitate to blow that pretty head from here to kingdom come if you'll not open your purse," he rumbled in ominous tones, waving his musket dramatically.

"I see," said Cat with slow deliberation, "but how you will contrive to do so without reloading that antique (for you have fired it twice, you know) I have no idea; however, I am sure we have no intention of discommoding ourselves further today. You may do as you please, but we shall drive on — and I assure you my men shall now have *their* arms at the ready." With that speech, Cat turned her back on the flustered bandit and was about to reenter the carriage when the sound of yet another horseman could be heard approaching at a gallop. This was beginning to be quite a curious day, Cat decided.

"Flee while you may, villain! Flee or meet a bloody death!" the advancing rider called out, firing *his* musket and waving it wildly about. Indeed, Cat felt a good deal more apprehension at the ineptitude of this apparent rescue than she had at the attack which had seemingly occasioned it. As this latest horseman charged forward in a suffocating cloud of dust, the first uttered a gasping curse, turned his mount, and escaped over the brow of the hill at the best gallop his sorry beast could manage.

Opening the door to her carriage, Cat leaned inside and announced, "Deliverance appears to be at hand, ladies. Feel free to compose yourselves." Caesar and Brutus, however, taking full advantage of the open door, now flung themselves through it furiously just as the second rider reined in amidst them. Belatedly assuming the roles of fierce protectors, the two dogs wove tight circles around and through the horse's hooves, barking incessantly, and causing the poor creature to rear and throw his hapless rider. This accomplished, the two canine heroes now busied themselves with worrying and tearing at the clothing of the newcomer who was crying out in some distress.

"Caesar! Brutus! Back at once," Cat commanded, but, as usual, it took the combined efforts of the occupants of both carriages, who were now in no small amount of agitation and confusion, to catch the two well-intentioned canines and confine them once again.

When that situation was under control, Cat had the opportunity to size up their would-be rescuer who sat in the dirt clutching at his ankle in unfeigned agony. His curious feathered hat had slipped to one side revealing sandy-colored hair and regular, if undistinguished, features. Tom and Martin had now come to his aid and were attempting to raise the gentleman up from his prone position.

"Have you been harmed, my lady?" the gallant managed to sputter.

"I am sorry, sir," Cat said, suppressing a smile, "but all the harm appears to have been done to you. You must allow me to make amends for the damages my wretched dogs have caused. We are not three miles from the inn where we stopped last night. Martin will lead you and your horse back there and see that an apothecary is called. Then we shall be on our way again."

"But surely you cannot travel this treacherous way on your own!" he protested weakly. "You must allow me to accompany you!"

"I think we are in no danger from that poor excuse for a bandit, and besides, my drivers are now alerted. No doubt we shall proceed unmolested now. But whom have we to thank for our gallant *attempted* rescue?"

"I am Geoffrey D'Ashley, at your service," he announced stiffly, much put out at her sarcastic tone. However ludicrous Cat deemed this gentleman, it was clear that both Audrey and Betsy were taken with his attempted chivalry, for they both stood open-mouthed, hands clasped dramatically against their hearts.

"Well, I thank you very much indeed," Cat told him tersely, "but it appears you would be well advised to be at your own service for the next several days."

With a good deal of wincing and suppressed moaning, the gentleman was helped to his horse and Martin led him back the way they had come while the remainder of the party discussed this exciting turn of events. Cat did her best to reassure all of them, for Betsy and Audrey were quite caught up in their lingering distress and fluttering hearts; in her own mind, however, she was not at all sure what to make of this curious episode.

"It was a madman for sure," Felicia declared, "but our Miss Cat showed him and no mistake!"

"Three cheers for Miss Cat!" Tom shouted. As the others joined in, Cat was very much relieved that this was apparently an unfrequented stretch of road. The last thing she wanted was the sort of sensational attention that an occurrence such as this might occasion, and she instructed her party quite plainly to refrain from discussing this event among any but themselves. This they promised with obvious reluctance, for it was clearly a choice bit of news to share with new acquaintances in London.

After Martin's timely return, they loaded themselves into the coaches once more and were soon on the road again. Eveline had held her peace until the relative privacy of their own compartment had been gained, before revealing her misgivings.

"Whatever do you make of this, Cat?" she asked. "I cannot believe it was all it seemed."

"No more do I," Cat agreed. "There was something exceedingly odd about both of those men. I feel as if I am on the verge of understanding it, but several very important pieces of this puzzle are missing. I do not think we were ever in much danger except from their remarkable bungling, but I shall be much relieved when we are in London nevertheless."

Eveline and Felicia could not but agree, and the latter directed many a backward glance down the road as their procession continued.

The rest of their journey proceeded without interruption, and it seemed no time at all until Martin was calling out sights of London, and even Tom, for all his apparent world-weariness of the day before, was nearly bouncing with excitement.

Cat had been to London briefly on several occasions, but found that she, too, was caught up in the thrill of the moment. Since it was still early in the day, despite the setback of the morning's adventure, Cat directed her coachman to take a more scenic route to the house of Lady Montrose, and the little party was treated to their first splendid sight of Westminster Abbey. While those in the first carriage were able to maintain their dignity with some little effort, an observer of the second carriage would have witnessed the sight of four countrified noses pressed eagerly against the windows.

As they made their way toward their destination along the blossoming borders of Hyde Park, all of the travelers made mental notes about the current fashion scene. The angle of hats, style of cravats, and presence or absence of walking sticks were noted by the masculine portion of the party, while the ladies remarked on shawls, sleeves, and, with a good deal of dismay, the sheerness of fabric of some costumes. Here, the reaction in the first carriage was no less shocked than in the second.

The afternoon had therefore begun to darken into dusk when the two coaches finally arrived at their destination. As the servants' carriage made its way to the side entrance, the other pulled up in front of Montrose House, a lovely brick town mansion facing on to a pretty square. The wide front doors were flung open to receive the little party, and they were met at the door by a tall, elegant, if somewhat aged, butler. Smiling pleasantly, he politely hid his dismay and overlooked the energetic antics of Caesar and Brutus who took immediate advantage of the central staircase to run an impromptu relay race.

"Good evening, Miss Mansard," he greeted her. "I hope your journey has not been too taxing. Lady Montrose is resting just now, but she has left instructions for you to be shown to your rooms. She will receive you in the drawing room before dinner. Would you care for some refreshment now?"

"Just some tea," Cat told him. "We shall be glad of a chance to collect ourselves before we meet Lady Montrose. Also, my terriers appear to be in need of exercise. Would you ask my Martin to collect them and take them for a good run?"

"Of course, Miss Mansard, I shall have them seen to immediately. Now, this way, please."

If Cat had entertained any commonplace notions of what to expect at Montrose House, these were soon shattered. As she, Eveline, and Felicia left the foyer and made their way up the staircase and through the halls, it became increasingly apparent that the furnishings were, if anything, extraordinary. The decor, Cat decided with growing alarm, defied classification. It represented not only a range of historical periods and taste, but a number of distressingly exotic cultures as well. Indeed, the ladies noted with growing trepidation a number of items, the purposes of which both invited and forbade conjecture.

Upon entering her appointed chamber, Cat stopped and held her breath. The room was lavishly draped with silks and brocades of various brilliant shades of rose and violet. In the center of the room stood the most unusual bed Cat had ever seen, intricately carved of some light wood, complete with sliding doors. The scent of jasmine hung heavily in the air. Cat turned to Eveline and Felicia, whose features reflected her own dismay. This house, she thought to herself with increasing alarm, is where I must make my debut as a model of propriety?

As the footmen carried in their trunks, the three women stood silently maintaining the expressions of frozen civility. As soon as the last footman had made his exit, they released their breaths simultaneously, sounding very much like three tea kettles about to boil.

"What in heaven's name do you make of this, Eveline?" Cat exclaimed as soon as the three were alone together.

"It is somewhat uncommon," Eveline returned judiciously. She cautiously opened the door to her adjoining chamber, stood for a moment taking in its wild peacock hues, and shut the door again. "I only hope, for your sake, that Lady Montrose's peculiarities, whatever else they may turn out to be, do not extend to her manners or person."

"Do you think we dare hope for that? I had sufficient reason to suspect Lady Montrose's tendency toward the outlandish, of course, but in the past her eccentric gifts were always a diversion. Indeed, Eveline, I am more than a little put out with fate for I would dearly love to enjoy all of this and throw concern for dull decorum out the nearest window."

"Well," Eveline sighed, "I cannot help but agree

with you. But take heart, Cat. Our fears may well be in vain, and there's at least as much to be gained as lost here. These rooms, although somewhat brilliant, shall we say, afford a rare showcase of the world's treasures. Here we are. Let us determine to enjoy ourselves as best we can!"

"If fears can't be allayed, we had best ignore them?" Cat smiled. "Capital advice, Eveline! Whatever would I do without you?"

"Oh, dear, Cat — look at Felicia!" Indeed, the awestruck maid was turning small circles, staring about her new surroundings with her mouth opened in the shape of an O. Had not the two ladies taken her quickly by the shoulders and set her down into a chair, there seemed but little doubt she would soon have spun her way right through the floor. Having secured the revolving girl for the moment, their inspection of the apartment was again interrupted by a timid knock at the door and a diminutive maid entered carrying a tea tray.

"Here's some hot tea, Lady Montrose's own brew," she informed them with a small curtsy, "and, Miss Catherine? These are invitations for next week — her ladyship thought as how you might like to look at them when you'd a moment to yourself. Can I bring you anything else?"

Cat looked over at her maid, who was still staring about bemusedly. "Take Felicia here with you — I believe the poor girl's in need of sustenance — and have her come to me again in an hour. Will that leave enough time before dinner? Good. Now what is your name?"

"Well, my real name's Sarah, but her ladyship calls

me Birdie, of course."

"Why is that?" Cat queried with some amusement.

"Well, to tell you the truth, I'm not sure I know, Miss Catherine. The fact is, she calls all of us maids Birdie, for some reason. And all the footmen are Matey. We're all just so used to it we don't give it a thought. I'll send your Felicia up just as you ask. Come along now," she said gently, taking Felicia by the arm. "Ring if you need anything, miss."

"Birdie and Matey?" Cat exclaimed incredulously after the servant had withdrawn. "What next?"

"Well, I own it does seem somewhat eccentric, but perhaps Lady Montrose has a faulty memory, and this system is easiest for her."

"Well," Cat returned, "I suppose as long as she calls me by my right name when I'm introduced, we'll suit well enough, but I've been Cat all my life and I'm hanged if I'll be Birdie!"

"You must remember that homely saying, 'Trouble not trouble, 'til trouble troubles you.' Now, what of these invitations? I am happy to see there are so many and so soon."

"Well, these are heartening, at least, Eveline. Whatever her eccentricities may prove to be, Lady Montrose at least appears to be received throughout London. Just look at these," she said, handing the invitations to Eveline one by one. "There is a ball in two days at Lord and Lady Hawkesmith's, a rout the very next night at the Marquess of Shrewsbury's, and three dinner parties the following week. Oh dear! We shall never have clothes made in time to go, more's the pity."

"Why, Cat," Eveline laughed in dismay, "I declare you are beginning to sound almost eager!"

"Well," Cat returned, coloring slightly, "I thought we had agreed that there is little to be gained by delaying a trial that cannot be avoided."

Eveline had been more correct than Cat would ever have allowed, however. A peculiar mixture of excitement and consternation were indeed building in Cat's heart by the minute. True, Montrose House, thus far, appeared to be fulfilling many of her worst fears, but it also seemed to offer the tantalizing taste of adventure.

Chapter Seven

As Cat and Eveline descended the staircase to dinner, they were indeed encouraged to find that the further they distanced themselves from the private chambers, the more conservative the fittings of the rooms became. By the time they reached the drawing room it was evident that any fears they might have entertained — at least as far as decor was concerned — were groundless. The exotic was confined off stage, as it were. The drawing room itself was furnished in the best of taste, hung with watered silk of a delicate sea green accented by arrangements of pink roses in silver vases. The ladies had dressed in the best of what passed for finery in the country — Cat in her lavender silk bridesmaid's dress and Eveline in a more sober gray silk. These would have to do for evening until they were able to engage the services of a modiste.

"Are you feeling more at ease now?" Eveline asked as they took in their surroundings.

"I am very much relieved," Cat allowed. "In fact, I begin to wonder if Lady Montrose shall not truly be the best answer to my predicament, for she seems to have mastered the art of maintaining a veneer of propriety over a host of idiosyncracies."

"Good evening, my dears," a small voice interrupted. "I am Lady Montrose." Cat and Eveline turned to see a fine-boned, elegant lady of childlike proportions. Her almost unlined face, set with wide china blue eyes, was crowned by a profusion of white ringlets. She was wearing a gown of fine pearl silk, caught at the sleeves and hem with rosettes of mauve velvet. Approaching them with hands outstretched, she smiled her greeting, "You must be Catherine. You favor your grandmother, dear. Alice and I were such good friends. I know that we shall be, too. And you are Eveline. Welcome to you both. How do you find your rooms?"

Cat glanced warily at Eveline, but before either could formulate an appropriate response, Lady Montrose's laughter, like the ringing of little crystal bells, broke the awkward silence.

"You must forgive me my self-indulgence, dears. Alice and I had a habit of teasing each other with such surprises when we were girls. Do you know, Catherine, your grandmother once dressed a monkey as the Queen Mother and let it loose at my twelfth birthday party? She did indeed. And in return, I hid that same monkey under the cover of a silver dish at her mother's next dinner party. I thought your great-grandmother would slide under the table with vexation. Ah me—how merry we were! You must count yourselves fortunate indeed, ladies, to have escaped worse than merely finding your chambers decked out like a seraglio."

"A monkey!" exclaimed Cat. "Are you quite sure?"

Lady Montrose smiled and fluttered her fan. "Well, no, to be honest, my dear, I am not *quite* sure. It may, of course, have been that Alice and I merely talked of doing such things. I've stopped worrying about accuracy altogether. It doesn't really matter whether it happened or not, does it? It's just as amusing!"

"But Lady Montrose . . ." Cat began.

"Lady Montrose indeed! You shall call me Mouse, as your Grandmother did. You, too, Eveline."

"I . . . we couldn't possibly," the two protested in unison.

"Very well, then," she sighed resignedly, " 'Lady Mouse' if you must be more conventional. Now, here comes Matey. Let us go in to dinner and you can both tell me all about yourselves."

However much Cat's fears for her future were heightened by Lady Montrose's various eccentricities, she could not but admit to herself that she also found them entertaining and endearing. By the end of dinner that evening, the little lady's good humor had won over her guests to the extent that neither of them would have traded her for a more conventional hostess, however much the future might depend on such. Moreover, the evening's conversation revealed that her ladyship's opinions and sentiments were all that could be hoped for and her peculiarities merely reflected a deep-seated love of the ridiculous.

They had returned to the drawing room for sherry when Lady Montrose's voice took on a serious note, "Now, Catherine," she began, "just what is this 'predicament' you were speaking of as I entered the drawing room earlier this evening?"

Cat and Eveline exchanged guarded glances and colored deeply.

"Come, come, Catherine," Lady Mouse continued, "we can have no secrets here, and I must confess I shall badger you until it's all out in any case. I own it is a bad habit of mine, but I am not at all likely to change this late in life."

And so it was that Cat, who was more than aware of her own lack of expertise as a dissembler, began to outline the strange turn of events which had brought her to London. Lady Montrose leaned forward and listened with avid attention, her brows knitting more and more closely together as the story progressed.

"And so it is, er, Lady Mouse," Cat concluded, "that you have our company this Season, but I own I am much happier about my fate since meeting you than I have been for some weeks."

"Thank you, my dear. I shall make efforts to see you remain so. I see now why you looked so distressed at our first meeting. Poor child! Saddled with such a burden to begin with and then to find yourself in such surroundings! Oh dear, it really is rather amusing, though, don't you think? I am exceedingly surprised at your grandmother, I must say, to have arranged affairs in such a terribly awkward way. She should have consulted me—I am sure I should have set her straight. Nevertheless, Catherine, I see you are a regular Wellington to face your difficulties so courageously and arrange your future as best you can. I congratulate you!"

Cat was much encouraged by this speech and plunged into a detailed description of the various preparations they had undertaken thus far. "Poor Eveline has spent much of her recent time as a slave to my deportment, with good success, I assure you. Now I have but to engage the services of a modiste and begin the campaign."

"I have undertaken to have Miss Spencer, my own seamstress, call first thing tomorrow morning, unless you had someone else in mind, Catherine," Lady Montrose informed them, "and I have already purchased some lengths of cloth that came in from Paris last week—although I fear they are not *quite* so colorful as those which adorn your chambers," she finished with a little twinkle.

Cat was more than happy to have been relieved of this last detail and thanked Lady Montrose heartily for her efforts. With affectionate camaraderie, the three ladies bid each other a good night and retired early in preparation for the challenge of the day ahead. Later, as Cat climbed gratefully into her elaborate bed, she took one last moment to look about her fanciful surroundings before snuffing her candle. It began to seem as if everything would be all right after all.

Chapter Eight

Although Cat and Eveline had each secretly looked forward with some enthusiasm to their morning appointment with the modiste, they were as weary of that pastime after some four or five trying hours as could be expected of sensible creatures. Their initial excitement was naturally heightened at the impressive array of muslins and silks and crepes displayed before them; nevertheless, the ladies' patience was soon tested by such pinnings and drapings and exclamations over color and style that each was heartily sorry they were not cozily ensconced in the library with a good book and a pot of tea.

When the trial was over, however, and freedom to move and stretch was accorded, they were well pleased with the morning's work, as well as the taste and ability of Miss Spencer, a good soul with a quick eye for accentuating the attributes of each to her best advantage. Moreover, Miss Spencer assured them that their first gowns would be ready in a remarkable two days' time so that some invitations might be accepted forthwith.

Midafternoon found Cat, Eveline and Lady Montrose engaged in a companionable coze in the library, their labors done for the day. Caesar and Brutus were assiduously performing such tricks as had won them treats in the past, all variations on begging winsomely (if persistently), and their little beards were disgracefully covered with cake crumbs and honey. Lady Montrose had entirely won Cat's good will by not only allowing the terriers to join their party throughout the day, but encouraging them in all their little antics as well.

More invitations had arrived with the morning's post, and with Lady Montrose's counsel, these were being considered both for the potential they offered of introducing appropriate acquaintances, as well as whatever chance of diversion they promised.

"Unless you enjoy close quarters, do not attend a crush, for they are aptly named," Lady Montrose advised them. "There is but little opportunity for conversation—just great crowds massing to be seen. Besides, the refreshments are disgraceful. No good in those at all. This musical evening at Branwell's should be just the thing, though, for they are good souls, if somewhat dull. We can't all be blessed with wit. It amuses them, however, to throw together such marriageable people as are of their acquaintance and observe the various stages of courtship. It is a near thing, perhaps, but your first gowns should be just finished in time. Now, I would avoid Almack's—indeed you may have no choice in the matter, for Mrs. Drummond-Burrell and I have had some differences over the years and my patronage would surely doom any hope of vouchers for you. In any case, I suspect you will be troubled enough by fortune hunters before we are done without seeking them out on their own turf, so to speak."

At that, a footman entered bearing a card on a silver salver. "What a lovely surprise," Lady Montrose exclaimed, taking it up. "I had no idea they were in town yet! Show them in, Matey. These are two special friends of mine—I'm so glad you both can meet them straightaway." Caesar and Brutus had pricked up their sensitive little ears and begun to bounce about zealously as the sounds of voices and footsteps drew near.

"Lady Mouse," came a familiar voice. "You are looking well indeed! Why Miss Mansard! I'll be bound, I had not looked for you here! And what's this? Caesar and Brutus! Champion!"

In recognizing one of the callers as Charles Hazelforth (the other gentleman was quite unknown to her), Cat's reaction hovered between pleasure and chagrin. Not only had she told that gentleman repeatedly that she had no intention whatsoever of visiting London, but she was also wearing that same muslin dress in which he had seen her so shockingly drenched at their last meeting. As soon as she encountered his eye, Cat felt her cheeks go scarlet.

A flurry of memories, both discomfiting and

delightful, flooded over her as she stammered a moment in confusion when he warmly took her hand in his. Cat was quite content to allow Caesar and Brutus to momentarily divert Hazelforth's attention from her as they danced noisily around his ankles, but through her downcast lashes she was able to confirm that his merest glance in her direction was still able to produce a mysterious flutter of emotions.

"Oh, you already know Mr. Hazelforth, Catherine!" Lady Montrose exclaimed. "What extraordinary luck! Do sit down, gentlemen, sit down. I shall order more tea and cakes and we shall have ourselves a nice little chat. Matey, take Caesar and Brutus here to the kitchen and tell Rene to fix them something special. Now, Hazelforth, do make Sommers known to the ladies."

During the niceties which followed, Cat was able to regain her composure somewhat, and soon learned that Hazelforth and Mr. Sommers, a friend from Oxford years, had only lately arrived in town. This latter was an earnest gentleman who was saved from looking overly serious by a wayward lock of hair which persistently found its way down onto his forehead. This he pushed back every few minutes with an unconsciously boyish gesture which his new acquaintances found quite appealing. The two gentlemen, it was learned, maintained a longstanding friendship of some intimacy with Lady Montrose and were frequent visitors to her house.

"Of course, it is always a pleasure to see our

dear Lady Mouse," Mr. Sommers began amiably, "but I hold myself fortunate indeed to at last meet Miss Mansard. Hazelforth has told me much of you." In spite of Mr. Sommers' innocent tone and open manner, Cat could not help but wonder just what information had been shared and, much unnerved, searched her new acquaintance's face suspiciously for signs of irony.

"We are discussing our calendar for the next several days, Hazelforth," Lady Montrose informed them. "I am just advising Catherine about Almack's — a dull and dreary den if ever I saw one. She had much better avoid it, do you not agree?"

"I am sure Miss Mansard's composure would be much overtaxed there, to be sure," Hazelforth replied with a knowing smile, "for I seem to recall that she has but little patience with the 'sorry simulations of society.' "

"And that is much to her credit you will agree, Hazelforth. However, I think we cannot avoid such encounters entirely, for the purpose of her visit demands a good deal of exposure. Pray, do not concern yourself, Catherine," Lady Montrose continued, on hearing a sharp gasp escape from Cat's direction, "for my seeming lack of discretion. Mr. Hazelforth and Mr. Sommers are my trusted friends, and it surely cannot harm your interests to take them into your confidence."

At this, Cat could only sputter helplessly, and Lady Montrose, turning a deaf ear to such choking sounds as emerged from her flabbergasted goddaughter, launched on a detailed explanation of Cat's situation and the mortifying circumstances which had brought her to London. During this narrative, Cat could but look wretchedly at the carpet while Eveline, no less shocked, silently commiserated as best she could, and sent sympathetic glances in her direction.

"So you see, gentlemen," Lady Montrose concluded, "my Catherine has her work cut out for her, and I am enlisting the two of you to help."

"Lady Montrose, if you please!" Cat cried indignantly, at last.

Ignoring this outburst, her ladyship went on, "Now, now, Catherine, you must surely see that the help of two confirmed bachelors will be invaluable to us, for they know far better than we the habits and characters of their fellows. Moreover, since they have steadfastly determined to maintain their single status, they have nothing to gain by either recommending or discouraging one alliance over another.

"You see, ladies," she went on, "I have worried myself no end these last two days: I have maintained some small position in society in recent few years, but not to the extent that I am able to advise you as to the character of any young man. I realize you must think me rash, Catherine, but I have a duty to not only promote, but protect your interests. Your situation makes you ready prey for the unscrupulous."

Here there was an awful pause in the conversation, filled only by the eloquent ticking of the mantel clock. Catherine and Eveline, who had already grown in their affection for the little lady, could hardly condemn her intentions; however, the mortification Cat felt (and Eveline felt for her) was overwhelmingly acute. Both Hazelforth and his companion, despite their gentlemanly polish, looked greatly ill at ease. Of the entire party, only Lady Montrose seemed in command of her emotions, and quite unperturbed by what she had done. The entrance of two footmen with the tea cart was, therefore, met with no small degree of relief, and the little party immediately made itself extremely busy with the passing of cups and plates.

The presence of the servants forced the conversation to confine itself to a stirring discussion of the weather, but the agitation of all parties, with the notable exception of Lady Montrose (who looked remarkably smug), was easily discernable on all their countenances. After a time, the gentlemen rose to take their leave.

"It has been good to see you again, Miss Mansard," Hazelforth told her with a bow.

"And, as you and Sommers will be aiding us in our endeavor," Lady Montrose reminded him, "I imagine we shall all be seeing a good deal of one another."

Seeing the blush this brought to Cat's cheeks, Hazelforth drew her aside and whispered, "Do not discompose yourself, Miss Mansard. Lady Mouse means well."

Cat was unable to meet his eye, for this sudden

disclosure of the galling details of her situation was almost more than she could bear, but she found the gentle pressure of his hand on hers strangely reassuring. Before their departure, the gentlemen sought and gained permission to call again on the following afternoon to take the ladies for a drive in the park.

No sooner had the door closed behind them, than Lady Montrose turned to Cat and Eveline and put her finger to her lips for a moment. Then she said, "Do not let's speak of this now, Catherine. I know you must feel that I have overstepped my bounds, and no doubt you are quite correct. However, I feel certain that time will see me vindicated. Now, if you will both excuse me, I have had an agitating morning and I shall have my nap."

On Lady Montrose's quitting the room, Cat spent some moments in silent turmoil, alternately pacing the room, throwing herself down on the sofa, and shredding her favorite silk handkerchief. Eveline, who knew that Cat was too sensible to continue long in this occupation, picked up her embroidery and waited patiently for her friend to collect herself.

At last Cat gave a great sigh, shrugged, and poured them each another cup of tea. "I can well believe now that Lady Montrose and my grandmother were ladies of a like turn of mind," Cat began as she seated herself. "Such meddling, however well intentioned it might be, is of the very sort evidenced by my grandmother's will in the first place. I do seem to be plagued of late by having my intentions thwarted and my pride battered about. It is a most distressing pattern to see developing in one's life."

"This is a sorry turn indeed, Cat, but not, I think, ruinous. But what of Mr. Hazelforth? Are you unsure of his discretion?" Eveline asked as she threaded a new shade of silk onto her needle.

"Of *that* I have no fear. We have had our little differences in the past, but I feel certain he is my friend and, if Mr. Sommers is his, then I can surely have no cause for alarm on that account. Once again, I am much afraid, it is my wounded pride which causes me the most discomfort. Oh, I do wish he did not know of my predicament, though!"

"Surely, Cat, Mr. Hazelforth can see that you have no choice in this matter," Eveline reflected. "You did not seek this awkward circumstance."

"Nevertheless, it is humiliating to be found out. For some odd reason, I had so much rather he thought my change of heart stemmed from mere whim, that I suddenly tired of solitary country life, rather than having been forced into actions so peculiarly repugnant to me."

"Well, I must agree with you then, Cat," Eveline told her candidly. "Your consternation does indeed seem to stem from hurt pride. Let us hope that that is all the harm this day brings."

Chapter Nine

The events of the following days were among those that, had Cat been an ardent rather than an indifferent diarist, would well have served to have been memorialized. Since rising from an altogether unsatisfactory night, Cat had become deeply apprehensive of seeing Hazelforth again. Her acceptance of his invitation to drive out that afternoon had been granted more from a sense of general confusion than a true desire to be thrust again into his company after so perplexing a meeting. She did, however, cherish a faint hope of restoring herself to his good opinion, which she feared must surely have been jeopardized

Cat spent the morning hours hopelessly tangling a piece of fancywork she had begun several days before. Such domestic undertakings had never held any fascination for her, and her characteristic lack of patience was responsible for her never having finished a single piece. Since coming to London, however, she had put her hand to one project or another in a more or less desultory manner as part of her attempt to project a conventional mien. Today's efforts were more disastrous than usual, for Cat's thoughts were quite taken up with what had passed the day before. From time to time, Eveline, who was quite dexterous with her needle, glanced at Cat's handiwork with a pained expression.

Lady Montrose did not make an appearance that morning, conveniently pleading some slight indisposition which confined her to her rooms, and Cat was, therefore, saved the anxiety a meeting between them would very likely have occasioned. Eventually, it was time for Cat and Eveline to prepare for their outing. Cat dressed herself with more than usual care in a gown of green lawn caught up with moss velvet ribbons. That very morning Felicia had found herself the unexpected recipient of the muslin dress which her mistress had worn the previous day and on but one other memorable occasion. When she cast it off the day before, Cat had silently vowed to never wear the garment again, and wished Felicia better luck than she had had of it. Eveline, whose wardrobe was a good deal more modest than Cat's, of course, wore a simple untrimmed gown of pale blue.

Hazelforth and Sommers arrived at the appointed hour in a barouche of ample proportions, and the little party was soon driving down the lanes of Hyde Park. It was a lovely blue day and Cat wished sincerely that her spirits were similarly bright. It was early enough in the day to avoid those who drove about merely to be seen, and Cat, for one, was happy to encounter few other parties.

Mr. Sommers and Eveline had found a mutual admiration for the works of Ben Jonson and were soon engaged in a spirited discussion. Cat and Hazelforth, on the other hand, listened in awkward silence. If only I had brought Caesar and Brutus, Cat reflected fretfully, at least we might have diverted our attention to them. She ardently wished to say something, but nothing appropriate came to mind. At last, Hazelforth addressed the driver.

"Pull to the side, John. I believe we'll walk for a while."

When the coach was stopped, Sommers handed Eveline down and the two continued their discussion, seemingly unconscious of their companions. Cat and Hazelforth followed them slowly onto a shaded lane and soon dropped behind the pair. They continued for a time in silence until at last Hazelforth said, "Do not be too put out with Lady Mouse. I know you would not have had your affairs known for all the world, but I am sure she meant well."

"I am sure of that, as well," Cat returned quietly.

"Miss Mansard, please do not look so cast down," he pleaded earnestly, taking her hand. "In this, as in all things, I am your servant."

"Oh, yes," Cat returned bleakly. "Your promise

105

of introductions and screening of suitors. I suppose we had best be about it."

"Of course," Hazelforth agreed with a sudden heartiness and briskness of tone. He had himself momentarily forgotten that commission and was glad to be reminded of it. The combined shock and gratification of becoming reacquainted with Cat had very nearly undone him. Since his quitting the country, he had held little hope of ever seeing her again and had philosophically resigned himself to that fate. Their separation had, in fact, been something of a relief, for never before had he felt so much in danger of having his affections at last engaged.

Miss Catherine Mansard had continued to occupy his thoughts, however. Only a few days ago, as he and Sommers had sipped their brandy and conversed into the early hours, their conversation had found its way to the topic of marriage. Hazelforth and his friend had for many years avoided that state, but from time to time they amused themselves by describing the sort of woman who might be able to tempt them.

"She must be beautiful, of course, and intelligent," Sommers had said.

"But not a bluestocking," Hazelforth had amended. "She must have a good measure of wit and good humor."

"Good family, too," Sommers went on. "And sensible. None of your swooning misses."

"In short, a companion," Hazelforth had mused.

"In short, a fantasy," Sommers had concluded.

But, for the first time, Hazelforth had wondered if his dream had come to life. Now that he had seen Cat again, he was even more confused. As he recalled their discussion now, the unspoken parallels he had drawn between his ideal and the lady whose image had so persistently haunted his leisure hours rose up once again.

Hazelforth pulled himself sternly from his dangerous musings. "Lady Montrose," he continued, "was quite correct in her assessment. While I have maintained a steady devotion to bachelorhood over the years, I am well acquainted with the characters and reputations of most of those gentlemen who consider themselves to be on the market, shall we say."

At this, Cat colored and cried out, "What a vile characterization. I shall thank you very much not to use that term with me, Mr. Hazelforth!"

"You must forgive me for being indelicate, Miss Catherine," he told her implacably, "but your situation surely calls for plain speaking. Now, I am more than pleased to advise you, as Lady Montrose has so wisely suggested, and before the Season is much older your dilemma shall be resolved. Yes, I can well picture it: we shall see you safely returned to your precious Sparrowell Hall, an appropriately grateful bridegroom at your side, plans for doing up the nursery ticking away inside your heads. Just trust me and we shall manage it all nicely."

Cat found the portrait painted by this hearty

little speech so dismal an addition to her already despondent mood that she was forced to bite her lower lip quite painfully to keep it from trembling.

"Come, come, Miss Mansard," Hazelforth chided as he watched her expression darken. "Yours is no worse a fate, indeed much better, than that suffered by many a young lady. Now Sommers and I have contrived an invitation to the gathering at Branwell's tomorrow night, so I shall begin my campaign then. Perhaps it shall not be so trying as you imagine."

Catherine looked at him in dismay. What sort of friendship was this? How could he be so cavalier in speaking of her predicament? And why, she wondered, was she so utterly undone by his indifference?

Hazelforth merely smiled and patted her hand. "Do you trust me in this matter?" Cat nodded glumly. "Good, then. Leave everything to me. Now dry your eyes, for here come Sommers and Miss Bartlett. They must have worn out poor Jonson entirely."

The foursome completed their drive to a large degree in silence, their minds taken up agreeably or not by what had just passed. Cat noticed that Eveline looked in excellent spirits and reflected listlessly that there was no match for a good literary discussion.

Cat's much beleaguered spirits lifted somewhat at the arrival of their new gowns the next afternoon, although she would have been much annoyed had anyone accused her of allowing such a superficial event to affect her one way or the other. Indeed, her temper had been so ruffled of late that even delving into a new novel had brought her no respite. Now, she and Eveline watched impatiently as Felicia ceremoniously undid the wrappings. However, unable to control themselves, they were soon up to their elbows in tissue. Cat's gown was of white silk, minutely figured with embroidered butterflies. Eveline's was a jonquil-colored moire with an overskirt of openwork green lace.

"Surely this isn't the fabric we decided on for my gown, Cat?" Eveline protested.

"But it *is* the fabric you preferred, is it not?"

"It is very lovely," Eveline sighed, "but it seems hardly the thing for a companion. I would not want to excite criticism."

"Well, Eveline, I hardly think it anyone's business in what capacity you happen to accompany me. For all they know, we are merely friends. Lady Montrose did not mention it in all her other revelations and I doubt Mr. Hazelforth will allude to it. It is an exquisite gown. Wear it in good spirits."

"You will look lovely, Miss Bartlett," Felicia added, "and I am sure Mr. Sommers will think so, too." At this Eveline colored and Cat looked quickly at her. How vexing of Felicia to imagine more than she ought!

Lady Montrose had rallied herself for the

evening's activities and she stood at the bottom of the stairs as they descended, looking very much like a gauzy, beribboned bonbon. "Lovely, my dears," she exclaimed, "I hope you do not mind, Eveline, that I interfered in your fabric selection. This suits you infinitely better. Now then, I have a little something for each of you, for I feel I must do something to make amends for my meddling, although I own I don't repent it."

With that she handed each of them a small parcel. In hers, Cat found a pearl-and-gold choker; in Eveline's was a topaz pendant. It was clear that each had been selected expressly for the gowns they wore tonight.

"I am just thinning out my collection, of course. I've not worn these in ten years and I should like to see them by candlelight once again. Besides," Lady Montrose continued hastily, "I have given you cause to think of me with less goodwill than you might, and I always find there's nothing like a sparkly bauble or two to smooth over little differences of opinion. And you will see I was right in the long run anyway."

Neither lady was deceived by the casual tone of this little speech, and they embraced her sincerely with considerably more charity than they might have done on the previous day.

"Now, now, put them on and we shall be on our way. Matey, is the carriage here? Lovely! Then ask one of the Birdies to fetch our cloaks."

* * *

Sir John Branwell and his lady greeted their party with good-natured enthusiasm. They appeared to be a kindly pair, but, as Lady Montrose had earlier noted, hardly scintillating. From the foyer, Cat's party could see into the salon where the assembled group was listening with perfunctory attention to a madrigal performed with less accuracy than animation by two pretty sisters and their prettier cousin.

"Yes, the Collins girls," Lady Branwell confided in a loud whisper. "They are sweet little things, to be sure, but no fortune to speak of. Bascombe there is quite smitten with Miss Collins, but his family won't hear of an attachment. What fun we shall have if they elope! Now the cousin, Lucinda Moreland, was to have wed the young Marquess of Halmore, or so it was rumored last Season. But here she is again. Ah, well, so it goes."

While this gossip might ordinarily have held some small interest, Cat could not but shudder at the prospect of herself being the subject of such whisperings in the months to come. Just then, she spied Hazelforth and Sommers enter and approach their party.

"Ah," Lady Branwell confided in an excited undertone, "here come two who have escaped unscathed for years, but perhaps the time has come for them to relinquish their bachelorhood at last. Mr. Hazelforth! Mr. Sommers! Do come here! How good to see you. Now you already know Miss Mansard and Miss Bartlett, and Lady Montrose, of course. Lovely! Then I must leave you to each other, for here come Mrs. Bellairs and her charming nephews."

Cat's party watched with some amusement as the determined Lady Branwell guided the hapless Bellairs none too subtly in the direction of the Misses Collins who were smiling in response to the scattered applause. When she was well out of earshot, Lady Montrose at once addressed Hazelforth in a low whisper, "Tell us what you see now, Hazelforth. Any prospects?" Cat began to fan herself furiously as she felt a deep blush creep over her.

"Let me see," Hazelforth murmured as he contemplated the crowd. There was, for the moment, an interval during which the guests milled about or addressed themselves to the refreshments. "Well, well. There's Monte Whiteside. No. No good at all. Three years worth of gambling debts. In any case, I recall Miss Catherine has no tolerance for dandies. And, of course, young Abelwhite. Good family, but a rascal by all accounts. Rumors of a duel last Season. Amberleigh—no. Sutcliffe—most definitely not! Ah, here we have it! Sir Harold Talbot. A widower, good fortune, unimpeachable reputation, and advanced enough in years to have become settled in his habits. Let me see if I can contrive an introduction. Sommers, help Lady Montrose and Miss Bartlett to the refreshments. Come with me, Miss Catherine, and we shall begin."

Sir Harold turned out to be a man of late middle age, somewhat portly, but apparently good-

The Publishers of Zebra Books Make This Special Offer to Zebra Romance Readers…

AFTER YOU HAVE READ THIS BOOK WE'D LIKE TO SEND YOU 4 MORE FOR *FREE* AN $18.00 VALUE

NO OBLIGATION!

4 FREE BOOKS

TO GET YOUR 4 FREE BOOKS WORTH $18.00 — MAIL IN THE FREE BOOK CERTIFICATE T O D A Y

Fill in the Free Book Certificate below, and we'll send your FREE BOOKS to you as soon as we receive it.

If the certificate is missing below, write to: Zebra Home Subscription Service, Inc., P.O. Box 5214, 120 Brighton Road, Clifton, New Jersey 07015-5214.

FREE BOOK CERTIFICATE

4 FREE BOOKS

ZEBRA HOME SUBSCRIPTION SERVICE, INC.

YES! Please start my subscription to Zebra Historical Romances and send me my first 4 books absolutely FREE. I understand that each month I may preview four new Zebra Historical Romances free for 10 days. If I'm not satisfied with them, I may return the four books within 10 days and owe nothing. Otherwise, I will pay the low preferred subscriber's price of just $3.75 each; a total of $15.00, *a savings off the publisher's price of $3.00.* I may return any shipment and I may cancel this subscription at any time. There is no obligation to buy any shipment and there are no shipping, handling or other hidden charges. Regardless of what I decide, the four free books are mine to keep.

NAME

ADDRESS _____ APT

CITY _____ STATE _____ ZIP

TELEPHONE (   )

SIGNATURE _____ (if under 18, parent or guardian must sign)

Terms, offer and prices subject to change without notice. Subscription subject to acceptance by Zebra Books. Zebra Books reserves the right to reject any order or cancel any subscription.

tempered and courteous. Nevertheless, Cat could not help but wonder at Hazelforth's choice for her. There were far more agreeable-looking men standing about, twiddling their watch fobs as they in their turn looked over the crowd.

"Ah, Miss Mansard," Sir Harold began, bowing over her hand. "Your servant. You hail from my favorite county, I believe. Dashed good hunting, you know, Hazelforth. I shall be at it again as soon as this gout's mended. Devilish bad business, gout. Tell me, Miss Mansard, do you keep a kennel?"

"I fear I do not keep hounds, Sir Harold, for I do not hunt . . ."

"Not hunt!" he sputtered in disbelief. "What, pray tell, does one do in the country if one does not hunt, eh? Sit about idle, eh? Do you ride?"

"Not at all well, I confess," Cat replied, taken somewhat aback by this interrogation. However, she took a deep breath and resolved to be polite. "I generally confine myself to strolling about the grounds or visiting my tenants, or else, on a rainy day, burrowing into the library with a good book."

"Ah, but a library ain't complete without a couple of good dogs at your feet in front of a blazing fire," he protested.

"Oh, Miss Mansard does have *dogs,*" interrupted Hazelforth, and he launched immediately into an extremely detailed description of Caesar and Brutus, as well as their various antics.

"You'll pardon me, Miss Mansard," Sir Harold

113

harumphed, but these two hounds of yours sound like useless, spoiled creatures. Don't earn their keep, if you ask me."

"I do not ask them to," Cat replied evenly, making an enormous effort to conceal her annoyance.

"If they were mine," Sir Harold pronounced, "they would starve till they brought in a badger, or a rat or two at the very least."

"Then, sir, it is a good thing their care falls to me instead." With that she excused herself with as much grace as she could muster. If Sir Harold were representative of London's eligible bachelors, Cat thought indignantly, she had best rethink her aspirations.

"When may I wish you joy, Miss Catherine?" whispered Hazelforth at her side once again.

"How can you think of jesting, Mr. Hazelforth?" she scolded in a furious undertone. "I have depended on you here, and all you do is laugh at me. If that odious creature is your idea of an acceptable bachelor, then I vow I shall never marry."

"Have a care, Miss Mansard. It has been my observation that sentences which include the word *never* are always lies."

"As are sentences which include the word *always*," Cat returned. "Now, if you would expend your mental energies on my expectations rather than my choice of phrase, I should be very much obliged."

"Forgive me, Miss Catherine," Hazelforth bowed, looking not the least contrite. "I had foolishly forgotten your temper." Forgetting the mincing steps she had practiced with Eveline, Cat strode across the room like a field marshall, finally rejoining her party, who were chatting animatedly with Mr. Sommers.

As Hazelforth followed at her elbow, he wondered what had possessed him to bypass several likable bachelors of easy means in favor of Sir Harold. He had not really meant to vex Cat, but he was not anxious to see her affections attached quickly or easily. Cat was a rare individual, he told himself, and she really ought to take her time in finding a husband. She deserved to be happy in marriage, and the person who would make her happy must surely be as rare as she. It would not do for her to make a precipitous decision, but the headiness of the London Season often clouded the judgment of even the most sensible of persons. Yes, he would make it his business to put a few obstacles in her path if only to assure himself that whatever decision she made was not arrived at in haste.

"Whatever is the matter, Catherine?" Lady Montrose queried in a troubled undertone. "You really must not frown so alarmingly until you are in the carriage!"

"Ah, Sir Harold has just proved himself a fool," Hazelforth informed them helpfully. "He was so unwise as to question the worth of two Aberdeen terriers who shall remain nameless."

"That was rash indeed," ventured Eveline with a knowing smile, "for they have just lately shown their worth on the road from Sparrowell. They are a most courageous pair indeed."

At that, Cat could not help but laugh, and she recounted for the group's entertainment the ludicrous episode which had taken place on their journey to London. "Yes, my vicious protectors cowered in the coach until that would-be highwayman had finally disappeared and instead crippled our supposed deliverer."

Much to Cat's surprise, however, her tale was met more with expressions of concern and anger than amusement, at least from masculine quarters.

"Why was I not told of this at once?" Hazelforth demanded.

"I suppose because I did not imagine it concerned you," Cat returned in some dismay. The memory of the episode had grown more humorous as time had passed and she had not at all anticipated this sort of reaction. Neither could she fathom this man who seemed at one minute to display a cold indifference, the next, concern and friendship, and now, an annoyingly proprietary air.

"I'll warrant there's a good deal more to this business than you guess," Hazelforth continued, oblivious to her icy tone.

"Surely, Mr. Hazelforth," Eveline observed, "it is no more than the fulfillment of a wager by some indolent gentlemen with more time than good sense. If you had seen them you would know they could not be serious. I grant you it was provoking, even frightening at first, but I doubt we were ever in any real danger."

Here Mr. Sommers broke in earnestly, pushing his wayward lock back from his forehead, "You must humor our fears, however, ladies, and keep us informed if any further untoward incidents take place, regardless of how insignificant they may seem to you at the time. And certainly you must not even think of walking or driving without an escort. A footman is not sufficient. You must promise to call upon our services whenever you have need of them."

"Indeed, I shall see that they do, gentlemen," Lady Montrose agreed composedly. "You are probably very wise. But just imagine their not telling me such a diverting tale! I see I shall have to be much more diligent in my inquiries." On hearing this remark, Cat and Eveline could but quake inwardly.

At this point, the music rose up once more and a group began to form a little country dance at one end of the room. Much to Hazelforth's marked annoyance, Cat's hand was eagerly sought by the aforementioned Mr. Abelwhite whose introduction had, after all, been unavoidable in a gathering so select.

To her mind, however, her new partner proved quite charming; he was not only rather handsome, but fawned on her every word, paying her many fine compliments. Cat was somewhat amused to note that the gentleman was exceedingly aware of his good looks, seeming to take advantage of every opportunity to display his very fine Grecian profile. Eveline's schooling had never before been put to such a test. Nevertheless, Cat was able to smile graciously at all of his foolishness and avoid the impulse to ridicule him as she might have done in other years.

How different his attentions were, she thought, from Mr. Hazelforth's brusque behavior. True, Mr. Abelwhite had been characterized as a rascal earlier that evening, and perhaps it was so, but at least he took some notice of her. Mr. Hazelforth had not even seemed to notice her lovely new gown, which she thought quite fine. And there that gentleman stood, she noted with rising irritation, scowling most disagreeably at them from the corner and looking as if his face would break.

"Miss Mansard," her companion was saying with a quizzical look on his face, "your thoughts seem much preoccupied tonight. I asked if you had been enjoying your stay in London."

"Oh, yes, indeed, although I have not yet had an opportunity to take advantage of all the city affords," Cat admitted.

"Then you have not been to Vauxhall yet? You must allow me to escort you there soon. The gardens are truly exquisite! And the entertainment — there is really nothing equal to it. Lady Montrose and Miss Bartlett must join us, of course. We shall make a party of it. I am sure they will enjoy themselves immensely. *Do* say you'll come." Mr. Abelwhite had by this time maneuvered her to the edge of the dance floor and was now holding her hand quite presumptuously.

"Why, I hardly know, Mr. Abelwhite . . ." The rather shocking reputation of those pleasure gardens had reached even the remote vicinity of Sparrowell Hall, and Cat hesitated for a moment, not knowing exactly how to extricate herself from this forward invitation. Just then, however, she caught sight of Hazelforth advancing in their direction looking exceedingly displeased. Suddenly piqued, Cat continued, "However, it does sound like a most diverting evening. Thank you so much for your kind offer. I am sure we shall all be charmed." Surely there could be no harm in accepting, she decided, especially as the invitation included the others of her party.

The particulars of their proposed excursion had been agreed upon by the time Hazelforth reached them. Cat, sweeping past him with a sweet smile, returned to the floor with yet another partner, leaving Hazelforth to mutter rancorous invectives to himself about the impertinence of disagreeable upstarts.

Chapter Ten

The next day, Cat was much surprised to find that Mr. Abelwhite had called while she was out on her morning stroll, as well as several of her other partners from the previous evening. She was even more astounded late that afternoon when she was informed by one of the Birdies that Sir Harold Talbot was awaiting her pleasure in the drawing room. Still somewhat unnerved by his odious pronouncements on dog training, she repressed a thoroughly unladylike groan. Quickly checking her toilette, however, she steeled herself to face his annoying presumption and made her way down the stairs, hoping his call would be a brief one.

"Ah, Miss Mansard," he greeted her heartily from the depths of an overstuffed chair. "You will forgive me if I do not rise. The gout you see."

"Indeed, Sir Harold, pray, do not discommode yourself," she told him as she entered, remembering to leave the door well ajar. Cat seated herself and exchanged a few pleasantries with the gentleman. Then, a stony silence reigned. Given his loquaciousness on the prior evening, she was at something of a loss. To hide her discomfiture, she began to stitch at a piece of Eveline's fancywork in a frame by the fireplace. Making even more of a muddle of the threads than was her wont, Cat felt a little guilty knowing that her friend must very likely duplicate several hours of work as a result of her meddling. When she looked up from this hapless undertaking, however, she was unnerved to see Sir Harold now staring quite boldly at her bosom. Worse, yet, when he encountered her shocked expression, he merely smiled.

Unable to bear more of his silent scrutiny, she blushed and endeavored to begin a conversation, "In this fine weather I imagine you must find your impairment most taxing, Sir Harold. Surely the call of the hunt must be beckoning to you."

"Quite so, Miss Mansard, quite so. But one has other considerations. Health, of course, and, ahem, social affairs." That little speech seemed to have taxed his conversational repertoire, and in the silence that followed, he returned to his silent contemplation of her physical attributes.

"Do tell me about your hounds," she ventured at last, desperate to turn his attention. Cat had, quite naturally, little desire to hear more of those creatures against whom her own darlings had been so disagreeably compared on the previous evening. She was, however, gratified to find that the introduction of this favorite subject at last unlocked Sir Harold's tongue, and the gentleman waxed poetic on the relative virtues of various breeds for a good twenty minutes or more.

"There is no finer beast in all of England than my Ruffian, I'll be bound, Miss Mansard. And I wager he would make short work of your dandified pair, had he the chance." As if on cue, Caesar and Brutus chose just that moment to bound into the drawing room. Finding an unexpected visitor, they were at once their sociable, if vexatious, selves, and were soon dancing circles about Sir Harold, begging to be made much over.

"Away from me, you scoundrels!" Sir Harold shouted aghast. "Watch my foot, I say!"

In a furious attempt to protect himself, Sir Harold made the fatal error of striking at the determined dogs with his walking stick. This action had little effect, of course, but to excite the pair further; Cat, however, who was much incensed at Sir Harold's bad-tempered aggression as well as his blatant ogling, had had quite enough.

Surreptitiously she took a ball of silk from the work basket beside her and tossed it with deadly aim in the direction of Sir Harold's tender foot. Caesar and Brutus leaped into the air for it — for "fetch the ball" as their mistress well knew was their favorite game — and landed directly and excruciatingly on Sir Harold's throbbing appendage.

"Damn and blast!" he cried out with an enormous yelp.

"Sir Harold, you make me blush!" exclaimed Cat, whose color was indeed heightened, but more from suppressed laughter than from offense at his language.

"Beg pardon, Miss Mansard," he managed to wince gracelessly. "If you don't mind, could you spare yourself the trouble to ring for a footman? I shall need to be helped to my carriage it seems. I'd keep a sharp eye on those beasts if I were you. What they need is a sound whipping, if you ask me."

"Indeed, Sir Harold," Cat returned in innocent tones, "I shall see that their efforts do not go unanswered. Now here is Matey to see you out. Good day."

When Charles Hazelforth called some minutes later, he discovered Cat still praising the little dogs and feeding them biscuits.

"Was that Sir Harold Talbot leaving just now? You must have made quite a favorable impression last night for him to have bestirred himself."

"I trust I was able to clarify that impression this afternoon," Cat remarked as she caught the dogs up in her arms and kissed each of them on top of the head.

"He did look somewhat disconcerted as he drove off. What was the matter?"

"Oh, I believe he *was* in some pain," Cat allowed innocently as she broke an iced cake into pieces for her little darlings. "Sir Harold suffers terribly from the gout, you know."

"And so shall those dogs if their diets are not

amended before long. City life does them little good, that much I can see. I called to see if you and these fat fellows would join me for a stroll. They look as if some exercise would do them no harm." Bending down to their level, he addressed them, "What do you say fellows? A walk?"

"Now that is hardly fair, Mr. Hazelforth," Cat scolded him as Caesar and Brutus threw themselves at once into a whirling frenzy. "You know very well that 'walk' is one of the two or three words they recognize. I shall thank you very much not to say T-R-E-A-T in front of them, or we shall be forced to take our walk in the pantry!"

As they strolled through the park's shaded lanes, Caesar and Brutus panting and tugging furiously at their leads, Hazelforth asked, "Now what of Sir Harold? What was the purpose of his call?"

"Why, Mr. Hazelforth, I can only assume he called in order to further acquaint himself with my charms. That was the general idea of my introduction to him, was it not?" Cat asked archly.

"I have had second thoughts, Miss Catherine," Hazelforth admitted gruffly. "I am not at all sure he is the proper gentleman for you."

"Why ever not, Mr. Hazelforth?" Cat asked with pointed innocence. "By your own admission, he is a single man of good fortune and character. What else should a woman desire in a man?"

"Nothing whatever," Hazelforth snapped irritably, "although I must say he did not appear to have left in a very romantic frame of mind. Or do all of your smitten callers exit swearing like sailors?"

Cat at last relented and recounted the highlights of Sir Harold's abbreviated visit, concluding with his painful encounter with the very creatures whose vitality he had questioned. Hazelforth at last seemed somewhat more at ease, and he laughed appreciatively.

"So his admiration is, I fear, to be short-lived," Cat allowed, "for I believe Caesar and Brutus will have destroyed any sort of interest he might have entertained. But it is all the better for the association to have been brief. You are, of course, quite correct in your assessment: Sir Harold and I would never suit at all. I wonder you should have thought of it at all."

"However true that may be, I suspect you have not seen the last of Sir Harold, in spite of the considerable hazards a continued courtship may portend for his much-abused foot. I fear he is not one to bestow his romantic attentions lightly, Miss Catherine."

"But surely," she protested, "he must see how little we have in common?"

"Come, sit here, and I shall explain," he directed, leading her to a little bench. When he had secured the dogs' leads to it, he continued, "Perhaps as far as tastes and sentiments are concerned, this would indeed seem an odd match.

But those niceties mean little in society, and certainly less to a man like Sir Harold. To his way of thinking, you and he are perfectly suited, amazing as that may seem. He was widowed before an heir could be produced, and you are young. He still hopes to expand his holdings, and Sparrowell Hall is a tempting piece of property. What's more, however little interest you may have in the hunt, that sport constitutes Sir Harold's most important reason for living—and the environs of Sparrowell, as you know, are unsurpassed for that pursuit."

"Drat the man," Cat fumed in consternation, forgetting entirely the polite simulations she had practiced. "However much my grandmother's well-meaning designs may have intruded on my expectations, such an alliance was not her intention nor is it mine."

"Come, come, Miss Catherine. Is not marriage a business arrangement for the vast number of souls who embark on it? Those who look for more ask a great deal."

"I do ask it," she declared, "and I shall have it. I refuse to be a mere commodity."

"Perhaps it shall not come to that, Miss Catherine," he said quietly after a moment. "There may be those who have been overlooked."

"Indeed there might," she admitted. She turned to Hazelforth, who was looking at her pensively. If only he were not so committed to his bachelorhood, she felt almost certain that she could love him. Their interests, humor, and sentiments seemed so compatible at times. But no, this was the man who was so anxiously seeking partners for her. Certainly, he had thrown himself into that mission with, if not enthusiasm, at least a businesslike practicality. It would be altogether too humiliating if he were to recognize her inclination for him.

For his part, Hazelforth regarded himself and his mixed emotions with equal consternation. He had never even fleetingly contemplated marriage, and never, since the days of his callow youth, imagined himself to be in love. Certainly, if the general mediocrity of each Season's debutantes were not enough, society offered sufficient examples of disastrous alliances to warn off any man of sense. And yet, here he was, acting suspiciously like a jealous schoolboy. The most practical thing to do, of course, was to find her a husband at once—if only he could overcome the anger that rose up in him whenever he saw her with another gentleman.

"It seems I do have another prospect. Mr. Abelwhite escorts me to Vauxhall next week," Cat went on, interrupting his musings. "He seems to me quite a likely sort, in spite of all your cautions."

"That rake!" Hazelforth protested. "You will do no such thing, Miss Catherine."

"I assure you, I shall do just as I please, Mr. Hazelforth! You are no relation of mine that you can command me in any way. Besides, the introduction you offered me turned out to be such a

127

dismal prospect, I have determined to form my own alliances. Now, whatever are these two fussing about?" she broke off, for Caesar and Brutus were indeed barking wildly and pulling at their leads as a familiar-looking gentleman leaning on a walking stick tried unsuccessfully to escape their attention. Cat recognized him at once as her would-be savior from the preposterous highwayman.

"Ah, Miss Mansard, so good to see you again," he mumbled, bowing awkwardly when he realized he had been recognized. "Geoffrey D'Ashley at your service, once more."

"Mr. D'Ashley! This is indeed a surprise and a coincidence. Allow me to present Mr. Charles Hazelforth. You remember my speaking of Mr. D'Ashley, do you not? This is the gentleman whose very valiant, if belated, efforts put our poor highwayman to flight," Cat said with an admirably straight face.

"I do indeed, Miss Catherine," Hazelforth returned, looking at D'Ashley as if he were some new sort of stinging insect which bore watching. "And surely, Mr. D'Ashley, you must remember Caesar and Brutus here, your partners in this daring rescue."

Mr. D'Ashley, they noted, was eyeing the enthusiastic pair with some marked wariness.

"How do you mend, Mr. D'Ashley?" Cat asked with all the appearance of solicitude.

"Remarkably well, I am happy to say," he returned, sounding anything but happy. "And you,

Miss Mansard? I trust you have not fallen prey to any disorder of the nerves as a result of that unhappy encounter."

"I, too, have recovered remarkably," Cat told him with an amiable smile. Then looking willfully at Hazelforth, she continued, "Indeed, you must soon wait on me at Montrose House. I am certain my godmother would be grateful for an opportunity to thank you herself for your part in our delivery."

Mr. D'Ashley, looking somewhat nonplussed at this attention, bowed once again by way of answer and Hazelforth, now quite red in the face with vexation, seized the canines' leads and, taking brusque leave of their acquaintance, firmly guided Cat down the path and through the park the way that they had come.

"How can you be so headstrong?" he fumed at her. "You know absolutely nothing of this man. He could well be dangerous, and I am certain he means to do you some mischief. That is quite the stupidest thing I have seen in many a day."

"You may keep your criticisms to yourself, Mr. Hazelforth," Cat returned sharply. "I shall do just as I please, and I shall thank you very much not to interfere further."

"You may certainly risk your own stubborn neck for aught I care," Hazelforth exploded, "but you have no right whatsoever to introduce such a questionable person to Lady Mouse's home."

Cat could indeed see the validity of his censure, and the justice of it stung her to the core.

Nevertheless, she was not one to readily admit an error in judgment. It was just as well, she thought huffily as they arrived at Montrose House, that there was no chance of a romantic inclination on Hazelforth's part, for each of them would very likely vie for the honor of murdering the other before their nuptials had long been concluded.

Chapter Eleven

Mr. Hazelforth left Cat at the door of Montrose House in what she considered to be a chillingly uncivil manner; indeed, he paused only a moment to scratch Caesar and Brutus under their chins before brusquely bidding her a good day. Had his demeanor been less forbidding as they left the park, Cat felt she might well have conceded her error in inviting the dubious Mr. D'Ashley to call. But I shall be *damned,* she thought wickedly, if I do any such thing now.

As Cat entered the foyer, she was greeted by an ecstatic Lady Montrose, who fairly pulled her inside the door. "Ah, Catherine, my dear, you have callers! Now don't worry about changing from your walking dress. Just go along in and greet them."

At the prospect of still more callers that day, Cat groaned inwardly and hoped that she could contrive to make the visit a short one. Gritting her teeth determinedly, she turned toward the drawing room. It was with a great deal of pleasure, therefore, that when she opened the door she discovered none other than Cecily and John, just returned from their wedding trip on the Continent.

Cat flung herself into their arms with an enthusiasm and affection equaled only by that displayed by the two little terriers. "Cecily, my angel! John, my dear! Let me just look at you. Lord, how I have missed you both! Now you must sit and tell me everything. Shall I ring for tea? No, I see you have some. Where is Eveline?"

"Calm down, Cat," Cecily laughed merrily at her. "I declare, you are acting just like me. Can London have changed you that much? Eveline is not here — she has gone riding out with somebody or another. Now, *you* sit down and have some tea with us. Our news is quite simple: the Continent, of course, is quite lovely, but I fear we have admired more great monuments, been lost in more cavernous museums, and stared into the depths of more dark paintings than even you and Eveline could bear. In short, we are come back to comfortable old England and are enormously glad of it."

"Quite so," John added with his characteristic succinctness.

During Cecily's speech, Cat had drunk in the sight of this pair. She had not known just how fond she was of this lighthearted couple until now. John looked much as he ever had, but Cecily seemed to have acquired a good deal of sophistication during her short time on the Continent. Her gown of azure blue trimmed in Bruges lace was elegantly styled and fit to perfection. Atop her golden curls sat a Victoria hat turned up on one side and ornamented with several ostrich feathers.

"I have just been acquainting myself with your charming cousins, Catherine," Lady Montrose told her with a smile.

"Oh, yes," Cecily chimed in, "and we are become old friends in just an hour's time. Lady Mouse and I shall be intimates before the day is much older."

At this, Cat reflected with amusement that it was a good thing Cecily had so little to conceal or she might well be reading the secrets of her young life in the pages of the *Daily Courant* the next morning.

"It seems to me, Catherine," Lady Montrose interjected, "that we must have some celebration in honor of your cousins now they are returned. What do you say to a fancy dress ball?"

"Oh, I should like that of all things! Cecily cried out before Cat could reply. "I could be a shepherdess all in pink ruffles, and John could be a dear rustic with a peaked cap and a staff! It will be great fun, don't you think, John?"

"Won't wear a mask, Cecily. Deuced bother, masks. Dribble my punch down when I wear a mask."

"Then we shall just wear little dominoes, my love. You see, Cat, John is just as excited as I am! I shall set about ordering my costume immediately. What a grand time we shall have!"

"I believe we can have all the arrangements made and entertainments devised in two weeks' time, if we put our heads to it," Lady Montrose continued, toying speculatively with her lorgnette. "I shall speak to Matey this very day. If we open the doors into the conservatory and out from there into the orangeries, we should have room for thirty couples. That would be just the right size, don't you agree, Cecily?"

As the two ladies began to plan the upcoming festivity, Cat could not help but feel somewhat superfluous to their gaiety and turned to John who sat quietly by, basking in his wife's energies.

"It seems we are to leave you no peace at all in which to enjoy your homecoming, John. Tell me, have you taken a house?"

"Indeed, we are not five minutes' walk from here, Cat, so you and Cecily can contrive your visits most conveniently. We are fortunate in having such ready access to our families, for my parents are here, as well as my cousin Hazelforth, I hear from Lady Montrose." Here John paused significantly, and it was clear that he meant her to say something, but she knew not what. She was sincerely tired of explaining her situation, as well as disturbed by the role Hazelforth had taken.

Luckily, she was saved the annoyance of relating the particulars, for Cecily broke in, "My parents have told me of your predicament, Cat. What a nuisance! I know it must be hard on you, but do not worry. We shall help you make the best of it, I promise. Besides, I believe this costume ball should be the very thing to divert you from your troubles."

"I fear I have all too much diversion of late," Cat replied wryly. "I don't believe I have had an entire evening to myself since I arrived! Tonight there is a dinner party. A ball on the weekend and next week we are all engaged to go to Vauxhall Gardens with Mr. Abelwhite."

"Vauxhall Gardens!" Cecily exclaimed with a laugh. "How decadent! However will you contrive to read your latest novel in such dim light?"

"Perhaps I can impose upon Mr. Abelwhite to hold my lamp! Do please meet us there, both of you," Cat begged, "for we have a great deal to catch up on. Your enthusiasm for the Continent is not what mine might be, but I should love to hear of your travels in any case. Besides, I gather I shall need all the daunting presence of my family if our Mr. Abelwhite is truly the rogue Mr. Hazelforth paints him."

John, who had not seen Cat deliver a good verbal trouncing in some time, pronounced the proposed outing a capital idea. Lady Montrose, on the other hand, now begged off, owning that she had much rather avoid the night air as long as she knew Cat would be adequately attended. John and Cecily soon took their leave as they had a number of other calls to make, but promised to join the party at Vauxhall the following week, as well as pledging to dine often at Montrose House in the days that followed.

Indeed, those days were so taken up with engagements and Cat's attention was so arduously engaged by her new concentration on decorum that she hardly felt herself. It was, as she told Eveline, as if someone else altogether had assumed her life and her true personality was moldering away unused on some dark shelf. Under civility's deadening influence, one smiling face blended into another, and Cat vowed that she could hardly tell one new acquaintance from another, nor even distinguish her own personality from theirs. Hazelforth and Sommers often helped make up their party, but Cat's attention was so often engaged by her endeavors and Hazelforth remained so aloof that they found little time to converse. Time, however, passed in a heady reel, and soon the evening of their excursion to Vauxhall arrived.

If Mr. Abelwhite had formulated any designs on Cat, he was soon forced to rethink his stratagem, for, in spite of the initial promise suggested by Lady Montrose's absence, the size and composition of Cat's party proved to be daunting indeed.

He had called just as dusk was beginning to deepen, and very gracefully bowed the ladies into his waiting barouche, paying them many fine compliments. Had either of the ladies been called upon to express a candid opinion, they, too, would have been forced to agree with Mr. Abelwhite that they did indeed look charming. Cat was dressed in a gown of fine silver gauze over a midnight blue, accented by silver spangles woven into her hair; Eveline wore a gown of subdued heliotrope edged with pearl silk.

While Cat was well aware of the reputation of Vauxhall Gardens as a place where unbridled flirtation, intrigue, and worse held sway, she was unprepared for the very real beauty of the place which greeted them when their carriage arrived. The gardens, which were in full bloom, filled the air with a heady aroma and were lit by thousands of small lamps making the landscape a veritable fairyland. The strains of a small orchestra filtered through the trees, accompanied by the slight tinkling of crystal goblets and the echoing laughter of coquettes.

Mr. Abelwhite led the ladies to a small pavilion he had reserved and ordered champagne and ices to be served, but before long Cat and Eveline were very much disconcerted to find that a number of quizzing glasses turned upon them as they took their seats.

"Ah, ladies, you are much noticed tonight. Well, that is no surprise, for you are both vastly more handsome than any others in the gardens. I am quite sensible of the privilege of your company, you may rest assured," Abelwhite told them with an ingratiating smile. Cat and Eveline, who were already becoming quite annoyed with his excesses, merely nodded as civilly as they could and addressed themselves instead to the champagne which was, according to Mr. Abelwhite, the only beverage available to alleviate the warmth of the evening.

A good many gentlemen of Mr. Abelwhite's acquaintance contrived to pass by their pavilion in the first half hour after their arrival. While Cat was unable to articulate the nature of her misgivings at these introductions, she could not help feeling very much like a prize pony at the fair, so closely was she scrutinized. It would indeed have surprised her very little had one of them expressed a desire to examine her teeth. Soon enough, Cat found herself inexpressibly weary of their superficial conversation, and she allowed her attention to wander idly to the crowd assembled about them.

The concept of Vauxhall Gardens had always appealed to Cat's democratic notions, for admission was only limited by the ability to pay a nominal fee. Nevertheless, it was quite shocking to see, at tables not far removed from their own, indisputable members of the demimonde. Moreover, these ladies in their scandalously sheer gowns and plunging necklines were all too clearly reveeling in their irreverent condition.

Cat had never been one to condemn a fallen woman; on the contrary, she had incurred the censure of a number of her more pious neighbors when she had imposed her will upon her uncle and insisted that female members of the staff who had found themselves with child must be supported through their difficulties and allowed to remain at the Hall. Nonetheless, Cat had always associated any fall from grace with an accompanying sense of remorse. These ladies displayed nothing of the kind, however, and were, to all appearances, enjoying themselves and the attentions of their masculine compatriots immensely. Noting Eveline's heightened color and downcast eyes, Cat began to feel quite contrite about their presence, and she regretted her headstrong acceptance of Mr. Abelwhite's invitation.

"Drat the man!" Mr. Abelwhite's bad-tempered exclamation broke through Cat's reflections. "Here comes that tedious Sir Harold Talbot. Whatever does he mean, following us here?"

Cat could hardly imagine a person more out of place at Vauxhall Gardens unless it were Parson Tweedle, but there indeed was Sir Harold being carried toward their pavilion in a sedan chair.

"Miss Catherine! This is indeed a pleasure. And Miss Bailey, is it? Bartell? Bostich?"

"Miss Bartlett," Cat corrected him through clenched teeth.

"Of course. Just what I said. Miss Bartley. Abelwhite, help me down here. There, careful now. Ah, an empty chair! Good show! Slowly, slowly, don't drop me all at once," he cautioned as he slid into the seat just vacated by Mr. Abelwhite. "There now. Where are you sitting, Abelwhite? You can't just stand around gaping like a trout—go and find yourself a chair."

Mr. Abelwhite, much disgruntled at this turn of events, cast a petulant look in Sir Harold's direction and went to find an attendant.

"You are looking quite well, Miss Catherine. Healthy color. Clear eyes. All of that. No unmanageable dogs skulking around, eh?" With that, Sir

Harold indulged in a short, mirthless laugh.

"I do hope you are feeling better, Sir Harold," Cat remarked with studied sweetness. "I was just saying to Miss Bartlett yesterday, I don't have the least idea what came over my dear little criminals. They are usually so submissive."

At this remark, Eveline was forced to turn away and cough into her handkerchief in a very suspicious manner. Sir Harold, however, was oblivious to the irony of Cat's remarks and launched recklessly into a lecture on the stringent training to which he submitted his own hounds. "First thing they must learn is absolute and total obedience," he expounded. "Whatever I tell 'em to fetch, they must try with all their might to comply. I recollect Bounder as a pup, tugging away at a pair of andirons with all his might."

"You mean you set them impossible tasks! How can you be so excessive?" Cat exclaimed.

"Good for 'em," Sir Harold grunted, beaming at his own expertise. "Give me a month or two with your rascals and you'd not know 'em."

"Indeed," Cat responded, horrified at such a prospect, "I don't imagine I should."

Sir Harold helped himself liberally to the refreshments and refilled the glasses all around. Cat, who by now had drunk considerably more champagne than she was used to, had been looking rather hazily through the crowd for the arrival of John and Cecily; she now spotted them among the advancing throngs and caught their attention. She was dismayed but a good deal gratified to see that they were accompanied by both Hazelforth and Mr. Sommers, who were able to arrange additional chairs to be brought with a good deal more efficiency than Mr. Abelwhite was apparently capable of mustering.

The champagne was responsible for at least a momentary softening of her recent animosity toward Hazelforth, and Cat found herself hoping that the evening would offer an opportunity to mend the rift in their relationship. True, she did not appreciate his meddling, but she did, after all, value his friendship.

"Sit down, sit down," Sir Harold invited them, pouring Mr. Abelwhite's champagne all around and ordering more. "Good of you to join us here."

"Why, Cat," Cecily exclaimed, looking about, "wherever has your Mr. Abelwhite gone?"

"That numbskull puppy!" Sir Harold interjected with a scornful chortle. "Young fool didn't have a chair. Standing around like an idle footman, so I sent him off."

At this remark, Cat found that she had to bite her tongue quite soundly to keep from laughing out loud; this exercise was quite useless, however, when Mr. Abelwhite did return. For though an attendant was indeed following him with a chair, the pavilion was by now so crowded with unexpected guests that there was no place for him in any case. The look of pained annoyance on his face was so comical that Cat and indeed, Eveline, were forced to turn away and hide their laughter under the guise of a whispered tête-à-tête.

Recovering himself quickly, Abelwhite greeted the newcomers and addressed himself to Cat, "Perhaps, Miss Mansard, you would care to take a short turn about the gardens. I'm sure you would enjoy seeing the main pavilion and the orchestra."

Both Hazelforth and Sir Harold looked so incensed by this invitation that Cat found herself willfully moved to accept it, and taking Abelwhite's proffered arm, the pair withdrew into the gardens. These were laid out so skillfully and with such splendor that Cat at first did not notice that they were not proceeding at all in the direction of either the main pavilion or the orchestra. As they threaded their way through the throng, Abelwhite pointed out this or that interesting personage, or called her attention to various favorite fountains or statues. Only when the press of the crowd grew less did Cat realize through her fogged senses that they were leaving the main thoroughfare and entering a more secluded and quite dark footpath.

"Mr. Abelwhite," she protested with some apprehension, "I fear you have mistaken a turn. Let us turn back the way we came."

Disregarding her hesitation with a short laugh, he steered her into a small, secluded courtyard. "Forgive my impetuousness, Miss Catherine, but I felt I must get you away from that noisome crowd. I have yet to see you alone, you know."

"Certainly that is as it should be, Mr. Abelwhite. Please, do take me back to the others."

Instead of complying, Abelwhite merely moved to block her retreat before continuing, "Pray, give me a moment. Since I first met you, I have longed to see you here in the moonlight. And here you are at last, shrouded in silver like Artemis herself. Pray let me worship at your shrine!" Had Mr. Abelwhite knelt at her feet after such a ludicrous speech, Cat would merely have been chagrined; she was, however, much alarmed to find that instead of that course he chose to fling himself at her with alarming energy, taking her into his arms.

"Great heavens, Mr. Abelwhite!" remonstrated Cat, shocked back into sudden sobriety. "Do stop this silliness at once and take me back to my party. Whatever can you mean by this?"

"I mean, dear lady," he declared in fervent tones, "that I adore you!"

"Mr. Abelwhite! Don't be such a looby! I have only spoken with you on three occasions. You cannot possibly adore me yet. Now unhand me at once!" she entreated as she attempted to disentangle herself from his embrace. Not at all dissuaded by her resistance, he continued to hold her and indeed to press his lips to hers as best he could, for she was struggling quite energetically. Cat had secretly enjoyed such scenes in novels, of course, but now found these untoward advances and lavish speeches far less pleasant in person than numerous swooning heroines had in print. Literary love scenes had clearly neglected some annoying aspects of such encounters, such as damp palms and labored breathing.

When she was at last able to extricate an arm from his hold she cried out, "I have given you fair warning, Mr. Abelwhite!" With that, she brought her fan down forcefully on his nose with a resounding snap. Mr. Abelwhite sprang away from her forthwith, crying out in pitiful anguish and holding his wounded nose in his handkerchief. Cat, who was quite unmoved by his moaning, turned unsteadily on her heel and sought the central garden as best she could, torn between fury and humiliation.

Chapter Twelve

Cat had no sooner reached the less remote regions of the garden than she herself ran soundly (and painfully) into the person of Mr. Hazelforth, who had apparently been making in her direction at some considerable speed. Now she stood rubbing her own nose gingerly as Hazelforth reached out to steady her on her feet.

"Miss Catherine! Come here and sit down a moment—you look frightful." Cat allowed herself to be led to a little bench which was screened, she was thankful to see, by the overhanging branches of a willow. Hazelforth looked narrowly at her for a moment, then gave a short laugh. "You had best take a moment to attend these spangles. They begin to look like epaulets."

On reaching up to her coiffure, Cat was mortified to find that her intractable curls had indeed fallen down during her struggle, and her silver ornaments were now very nearly resting on her shoulders.

"Now, tell me what has happened," Hazelforth

145

insisted after giving her a few moments to right herself.

Cat was beginning to feel not at all well. Silence filled the air between them for some moments before she answered faintly, "I have broken my fan."

"And . . . ?" Hazelforth pursued, growing impatient.

Cat bit her lower lip to stop the tears that now welled up, more, it is to be guessed, from consternation than remorse. Then she gave an unsteady sigh. "I fear I have also broken poor Mr. Abelwhite's lovely nose."

"Poor Mr. Abelwhite?!" he cried hotly. "If he has touched you, Cat, he will be fortunate not to be *dead* Mr. Abelwhite!"

"Why, Mr. Hazelforth, do you think it will come to that?" Cat asked in shocked dismay, her head beginning to throb ever so slightly. "I own, I had not thought of that at all. If he should call me out, may I name you as my second?"

Hazelforth laughed softly in the darkness and put his arm around her shoulders. "I fear you have consumed far more champagne than was absolutely wise, my little Cat. Have you had any dinner? I thought not. I fear I must insist that you return home at once."

"And if I choose not to?" she demanded querulously, lifting her chin with a stubborn tilt.

Here Hazelforth sighed heavily. "Miss Catherine, it is clear that the spirits have gone to your head tonight. Whatever prompted you to drink so much of that treacherous champagne?"

"Well," Cat sniffed, "the evening was so warm,

146

and they serve no other beverages here."

"Where on earth did you get that idea?"

"Why, Mr. Abelwhite assured us it was so. He was quite apologetic."

"Cur," Hazelforth muttered. "Trust me, Miss Catherine. It is best you return home at once. I doubt indeed that Mr. Abelwhite will call you out," he smiled, "for duels of any kind are now illegal, as you will recall. But I do fear he is not to be trusted, particularly if he feels his dignity has been affronted. Now, if for no other reason, you must return to Montrose House in order to avoid making a spectacle of yourself. You can ill afford it, as we both know."

Cat now found her senses returning to her with uncomfortable clarity, and she had to admit, albeit silently, that Mr. Hazelforth was quite likely correct. Taking a moment to repair her toilette as best she could, she allowed him to convey her to his carriage with unaccustomed meekness.

"I shall tell the others that you are suddenly indisposed. My driver will return for me later. Now, off with you!"

As Hazelforth watched the carriage disappear into the darkness, the anger he had held in check now surfaced in earnest. What Cat had not told him he could easily guess, for, in spite of her temper, he doubted she would ever resort to violence unless she felt her honor or safety to be threatened. Mr. Abelwhite, he vowed, would have more to worry about than the destruction of his profile.

Both Eveline and Lady Montrose had the good

grace to repress their curiosity the next morning, although Cat realized that what had taken place must indeed have been quite clear to them. Nonetheless, she allowed her throbbing head the greater part of her attention, keeping to her chamber for most of the morning.

When she finally did arise, she permitted Felicia to dress her like a rag doll and only winced a little as her hair was coaxed into some semblance of discipline. As Cat deliberated drearily over the choice of gown, Felicia crossed to the window and, hands on hips, stood staring into the park below.

"Tsk, tsk!" Felicia lamented in loud disapproval.

"What is it?" Cat asked wearily.

"Oh, nothing, nothing. But this is truly a wicked world, Miss Cat."

"Come now, Felicia, out with it," her mistress told her sharply. "It is clear there is something you wish me to know. My head feels too much like a pincushion to play games this morning."

"Well," the maid said with a long-suffering sigh, "see for yourself."

With a much put-upon groan, Cat made her way to Felicia's side and peered out the window into the painfully sunny day. Half hidden behind some shrubberies, however, Cat was very much surprised to see Mr. Geoffrey D'Ashley quite presumptuously holding the hand of none other than Audrey, her parlor maid.

"Surely that cannot be our Audrey walking about with Mr. D'Ashley! Did you know of this

148

connection, Felicia? Why was I not told of it at once?"

Felicia frowned and with a much aggrieved sigh explained, "Why, Miss Cat, you know quite well I have had more than one lecture from you about carrying tales from the servants' hall. I thought you would be pleased to find I'd finally learned my lesson."

Cat quickly dismissed her former dictates on tale bearing with a small shrug. "How long has this been going on?" she demanded.

"Almost since our arrival, and poor Betsy is that upset. Fit to be tied. *She* is the one used to having followers, being so pretty and dainty and all. And Audrey, Miss Cat! You wouldn't believe the insolence of that chit, queening it over Betsy, who was fair taken with Mr. D'Ashley from the first time she saw him. It is a regular theatrical belowstairs."

Had Felicia been more forthcoming in her descriptions, it would have been clear to Cat that the scenes which had taken place in the servants' hall of late had no place on a stage of any kind. The friction between the two parlor maids on account of Mr. D'Ashley's inexplicable attentions had grown from piqued vexation to outright animosity, and provided the rest of the staff with no end of diversion and conversation.

"Perhaps I should speak with her," Cat reflected, realizing that this untoward attachment very likely was the reason that Mr. D'Ashley had ignored her invitation to call, "but not until this wretched headache goes away. I fear I must be coming down with the grippe."

Felicia, who suspected quite rightly that Cat's indisposition stemmed from her indiscretions of the previous night, wisely kept her misgivings to herself and, feigning innocence, merely offered to have an apothecary summoned. This service Cat declined with huffy annoyance and she soon made her way down the stairs to the drawing room, where she found the subdued colors far more soothing than the dazzling shades of her own chamber.

For the first time in their lives, Cat shrank from the exuberance of Caesar and Brutus and, shuddering at each piercing yap, commissioned Martin to walk them until they were worn out and gave him fare for a hackney cab in which to return. Then she sank into a chair with a cool cloth over her face. As midday passed, Cat began to think she might contrive to remain among the living for at least the immediate future, and was able to face a light lunch of tea and dry toast. Her incipient vitality soon shrank, however, as Sir Harold Talbot hobbled into the room. He was closely followed by the butler, who announced him in an uncertain voice which bespoke his chagrin at this intrusion.

"Miss Mansard," Sir Harold exclaimed more loudly than necessary as he entered, "you are looking rather sallow! Had a cup too much, eh? What you need is a pint of bitters. The very thing!"

Cat could but wince at the thought and assured him that she needed no such thing, and privately added that a little peaceful solitude, if such a thing could be contrived, would set her straight before too long. Sadly, however, she had grown too accustomed to good manners in recent weeks to voice these honest sentiments aloud.

"It is good of you to call, Sir Harold," she said in tones she hoped would mask her true feelings. "Just a moment—let me ring for Lady Montrose or Miss Bartlett to join us."

At that, Cat was very much surprised and, indeed, alarmed, to see Sir Harold turn and close the door behind him. "My dear Miss Mansard, my dear *Catherine,* I must have some words privately with you."

If Sir Harold's recommendation of a pint of bitters had caused her head to spin, his next suggestion wrought even further damage. Taking care to arrange two overstuffed pillows on the floor in front of her, Sir Harold lowered himself with conspicuous discomfort to his knees and grasped her hand with hearty enthusiasm. Then, after a flustered pause of some seconds, he pulled from his pocket a piece of paper on which appeared to be written a list; he took a moment to peruse it, returned the paper to his pocket, then cleared his throat noisily.

"My dear Catherine," he began dramatically, "you must permit me to express my, er, deepest affection for you. It has grown steadily, er . . . like a . . . like a healthy bounding pup! That's it—I say, I like that! Like a healthy pup! My heart has pursued your own staunchly," he rushed on, warming to his subject, "like a good hound on a

151

blood scent. I can but follow its lead. And now I, er, . . . Oh, yes! Now, my dear," he went on hastily, "I must entreat you to become my wife. You hold my happiness in your hands. Do not disappoint me!"

Had Cat been feeling less afflicted, she might have found Sir Harold's proposal amusing. As it was, she forced herself with some difficulty to maintain her equanimity as her head began to throb violently once again.

"You are overcome with emotion, I daresay, my dear," Sir Harold chuckled heartily, misinterpreting her silence altogether. "I know how sentimental you females are. I cannot blame you, my dear. I must own, the thought of a pack of prime hounds and our seven or eight hearty children scampering about the countryside, hot on a burning scent, bringing home great piles of pheasants and quail, overwhelms me as well."

This last image so overwhelmed Cat that her stomach at last rebelled and she was forced to flee the room abruptly in search of a convenient basin. Unfortunately, Sir Harold was not only mystified, but, because of his own affliction, found himself stranded on his knees until a passing footman was able to rescue him.

By the time Cat had recovered herself sufficiently to return to the drawing room, Sir Harold had gone and Lady Montrose had taken his place. Cat was grateful to find that the little lady studiously applied herself to her needlework and did not endeavor to catch her eye or engage her in conversation other than to ask if she were feeling any better.

"I am, physically," Cat told her, "but I do not know how much longer I can contrive to maintain the good breeding Eveline has been such a slave to, if I am continually confronted by men who have none. I begin to think that living a life of genteel poverty is not such a bad thing compared to sharing a life of any kind with the company I have endured lately. And to think, there are another two months left in the Season. Surely, it is more than I can bear!"

"Well, Catherine," Lady Montrose soothed, "tonight we shall have a quiet family dinner, and we can be ourselves. Cecily and John will be here, and Hazelforth and Sommers who are quite like family to me."

The prospect of seeing Hazelforth so soon did little to console Cat, who recalled with mortification their last encounter. What a hoyden he must have thought her, she reflected miserably to herself, to follow Abelwhite into the gardens in that brazen manner. And whatever was all that silliness about Abelwhite calling her out? Perhaps she had just imagined it.

"I am afraid," Lady Montrose was continuing, "that you have not seen the end of Sir Harold Talbot. When he left he seemed to be under the impression that you had been overcome by the passion of his addresses and would confirm your acceptance verbally when next you met. I gather that Mr. Abelwhite's attentions last night have encouraged him to speak his mind more precipitously than he might otherwise have done."

"Indeed, I *was* overcome," Cat admitted with a blush of keen embarrassment at the memory of her precipitous flight, "but not, I assure you, by passion. I am sorry he so acutely misunderstood my predicament. Oh, dear! Is nothing ever to be easy again?"

"No doubt some day, Catherine, no doubt," the lady returned serenely. "Sir Harold is a determined man, but I have no fear you can eventually dissuade him in his suit. But, tell me, you have been here some time now and met a number of agreeable young men. Do you find your heart even a little engaged?"

At this Cat knew not how to reply. Her heart had indeed been quite full of late, but she was hesitant to interpret its agitation.

"What of Mr. Hazelforth?" Lady Montrose asked pointedly, breaking in on her reflection.

"Lady Mouse!" she returned with a flush. "You know quite well that Mr. Hazelforth does not consider marriage a part of his future."

"That may well be," she allowed, "but you still have not answered my question."

"Perhaps I do not know how to," Cat cried in sudden desperation, deserting her companion for the more secure regions of her chamber.

Dinner that evening did prove to be a welcome respite from the tumult that had surrounded their recent days. Cecily and John arrived together with Mr. Sommers, who explained that Hazelforth was seeing off an acquaintance and would join them later, a revelation which Cat met with mixed feelings, for she had begun to both anticipate and dread his presence.

As Lady Mouse conversed gaily with Cecily about their planned costume ball, and Mr. Sommers immediately claimed Eveline's attention with a new book he had brought to show her, Cat felt rather neglected. As in all gatherings, John smiled rather than conversed, and Cat found her attempts at introducing a subject for discussion something of a trial.

She had had very little opportunity to converse privately with Eveline since their arrival and was quite perplexed to see the extent to which her time was apparently being engaged by Mr. Sommers. Whatever could he mean by it? She sincerely hoped that Eveline's affections were not being engaged in more than an intellectual sense for, after all, Mr. Sommers was every bit as much a confirmed bachelor as Mr. Hazelforth. But as she watched them, Eveline's cheek suffusing with color as she laughed at some witticism from Mr. Sommers, Cat could not help but envy their easy friendship, whatever its depth. If only there were someone with whom she could be so tranquil.

Hazelforth arrived just as dinner was announced and Cat found herself quite flustered as he smiled at her with a kindness she had not enjoyed for some time.

"Why, Charles," Lady Montrose greeted him, "I must say you are looking well pleased with yourself tonight. Why so smug?"

"I have just seen to the exportation of some troublesome baggage," he replied cryptically.

"I thought Mr. Sommers said you were seeing someone off," Cecily protested.

"Why, so I was," he returned, offering her his arm as they went into dinner. Hazelforth did not address the subject again, however, in spite of Cecily's spirited entreaties throughout dinner that he satisfy her curiosity. As the evening was quite warm, Lady Montrose suggested they repair to the garden for sherry when dinner was finished. "In my home, when we are among friends," she explained, "I do not allow the men to wallow about in their port till all hours, forsaking the ladies to the ennui of their own tired companionship. Such a beastly practice!"

Cat could not but agree, for she had spent many a weary hour among bored females, only to be joined hours later by the gentlemen, sodden with alcohol and reeking of cigars. This was indeed a much better plan. Cecily and John sat chatting with Lady Montrose as she fanned herself with a palm frond; Eveline showed Mr. Sommers the orchids with which Lady Montrose and her butler had been experimenting in the conservatory. Cat descended a staircase to the garden and leaned against the cool marble balustrade, breathing in the night air. Looking up at the full moon, she shuddered weakly, remembering wretchedly the excesses of the night before.

"Are you cold?" she heard Hazelforth ask quietly from behind her.

"No. Not cold. Haunted with chagrin, I fear. Last night beneath the same moon . . ." she faltered.

"Do not think of it," he said softly.

Cat sighed in the dim light. "Oh, I know that a few months hence I shall somehow find the humor in all of this. But, Mr. Hazelforth, I begin to fear that I am incorrigible beyond all hope. Poor Eveline has been such a slave to my deportment. You have no idea! But at the least provocation my lessons desert me and I find myself not only on the path to compromise, but guilty of destroying a perfect Grecian profile. I do not know how I shall ever face that gentleman again, for I know our paths must eventually cross."

"That will be the least of your worries, Miss Catherine. I have spoken with that person today and convinced him that a year spent on the continent would be best for his health. I have just made certain that he was aboard the ship when it sailed."

"Why, Mr. Hazelforth! How did this . . . ?

"Please, Miss Catherine, think no more on that unfortunate encounter and do not berate yourself for your conduct. Your attack on that scoundrel was as well deserved as it was well aimed. You should be happy to know that your fan will be more easily set to rights than a certain swollen proboscis. Remind me never to offend you, my dear," he smiled at her.

"Oh, do not tease me, Mr. Hazelforth!" Cat remonstrated. "Besides, I am much afraid that my little ivory fan, which was a favorite, by the way, is scattered about in several pieces on a certain path at Vauxhall. Do let us speak of something else."

"Very well," he went on in a grim tone. "I understand another ardent suitor has not been so strikingly rejected. Sir Harold Talbot is sounding it about that you have all but accepted his suit."

"Sir Harold Talbot indeed!" Cat stormed. "The audacity of that tedious man has very nearly undone me. I cannot think how you ever came to set him in my path. Whatever possesses him?"

"The notion of possessing you, I should imagine. You are a fine quarry for a huntsman who fancies himself an exceptional catch as well. May I assume you do not intend to accept him?"

"You may indeed! Oh, Mr. Hazelforth, whatever am I to do? I comprehend the Season is still young, but I have yet to attract the attention of a man whose presence is not a punishment."

"Now, be truthful, Miss Catherine. Several times I have called to find my own card preceded by those of quite acceptable young men. They are not all Henry Abelwhites and Sir Harold Talbots. It seems that you contrive to be conveniently absent during the hours traditionally reserved for such calls. What is it you want?"

Cat looked at Hazelforth in the moonlight and felt her throat tighten. At last, she admitted to herself what her heart had known since the first: she loved a man who was beyond her grasp, a man would never be hers. "I want what I cannot have," she whispered.

"Is your independence so precious to you then?" he asked in an unreadable tone.

Of course that was what he would think, she told herself, and what he must continue to think.

Gathering herself, she replied with forced nonchalance, "You yourself must admit that the prospect of sharing one's life is not to be contemplated lightly, Mr. Hazelforth. You must concede that you have clearly valued your own independence. My decision has been taken away from me, but what would tempt you to cast your liberty aside?"

"What indeed?" he echoed softly, searching his heart for an answer.

Chapter Thirteen

Cat awakened from a troubled sleep and remained in bed contemplating her misfortunes as she sipped her cocoa. She seemed to be pursued only by those whom she wished to flee, and the man she loved was one she was too proud to pursue. It was all too unfair and too confusing. This reverie, however, was interrupted by Felicia.

"It's that Sir Harold Talbot downstairs, Miss Cat. I told him to come back later, but he vows he'll stay right where he is until he sees you."

Cat stretched and groaned in a decidedly bad humor. "Drat the man. I don't know whether to let him cool his heels for an hour or two or dispatch this wretched business speedily." As it was, Sir Harold was forced to wait a good hour before Cat completed her toilette and proceeded reluctantly down the stairs to face him.

"What's this? Sleeping half the day away, my dear Catherine?" he chided her by way of greeting. "That shall all change when we are established at Sparrowell, my dear, as shall some other things I have been contemplating since yesterday. I have been engaged in some investigation, and I am sorry to say I find your affairs to be in a shockingly sorry state."

"Do you indeed?" she remarked in a dangerously calm voice. Had Cat been more generously disposed toward Sir Harold, she would have stopped him at once, but an admittedly unkind curiosity prodded her to discover exactly what visions of reform she would shortly be destroying. Sir Harold had by this time taken yet another list from his waistcoat pocket and immediately commenced to tick off a number of items of concern.

"Now first, what's this about providing medical services for your tenants? Preposterous! A good epidemic now and again weeds out the bad stock. And a school for the village children? Not only expensive, my dear, but unwise as well. Gives them ideas, it does. Take a lesson from the Frenchies. Their leniency cost more than a few heads—not that a few thousand frogs more or less makes much difference to us. Now about those pampered mutts of yours. I shall undertake their discipline and retraining personally and shall immediately begin . . ."

At the introduction of this sensitive subject, Cat decided that she had heard quite enough for one day. "If you please, Sir Harold . . ." she began sharply.

"Eh, what's that?" he interrupted, looking up from his notes. "Ah, you want another proposal do you? Very well, but I shan't get down on my knees again, so you'll have to take me standing up."

"I should not have you if you stood on your head, Sir Harold!" she cried, much put out. "I have never heard such a bold, impertinent, noxious speech in all my life. Now you may fetch your own hat and walking stick and show yourself out, for I'll have none of my servants playing fetch for you. Good day, sir!"

Sir Harold regarded her for a moment in silent dismay before he turned to go. Whatever had he done to put her into such a pet, he wondered. Truly, there were no understanding females. Give him a good hound any day. Just before he exited, however, he turned and asked hopefully, "Not just being coy, eh, Miss Catherine?"

By way of answer, Cat seized a handy piece of bric-a-brac and hurled it furiously in his direction. As it smashed against the wall, Sir Harold made a hasty escape with amazing dexterity, considering his impairment. He had not been more than a few seconds absent, however, when Mr. Hazelforth appeared in the doorway, looking backward over his shoulder with clear amusement.

"I say, Miss Catherine," he began, as he made his way into the room, "is it your intent to maim all of your suitors before the end of the Season? If so, I feel it only fair to post a warning to that effect in front of Montrose House."

"Mr. Hazelforth, kindly refrain from vexing me further," she entreated him. "My patience has already been much tested, and the day is yet young."

"Believe me," he responded with a short laugh, "I value my good health too highly to test your temper further. However, I am here to see Lady Montrose this morning. Where might I find her?"

"I believe she is still in the morning room," Cat returned, somewhat disconcerted.

"Do not trouble yourself. I know the way."

"Well, Hazelforth," Lady Montrose greeted him, looking up from her game of patience. "I assume from the sound of broken glass I heard a moment ago that our heartless Catherine has sent poor Sir Harold packing. Is that a wise thing do you think? He is the only one to come up to scratch thus far."

Hazelforth looked narrowly at his old friend, trying to read her expression. As usual, it proved to be an impossible task. "I imagine," he said at last, "that she will have many other offers this Season."

"And will you wish her joy when she finally accepts one?" Lady Montrose asked him pointedly.

"I have and shall always wish her joy," he mumbled, thrusting his hands deep into his pockets and looking out the window into the garden.

"You are a fool, Charles," Lady Montrose said quietly.

Hazelforth turned and looked at her sharply.

"In fact, I am much afraid you are both fools," she continued, slowly turning each card. "Happiness is crying at your doors, and you stop your stubborn ears."

Hazelforth turned away from her again. For all of his recent daydreaming, it was time to face the cold truth. The only happiness he had ever found had come of avoiding marriage like the plague. He had seen too much sorrow there, too much cynicism, too much calculation. He had committed himself instead to safe friendships, lighthearted flirtations, and he had no need of anything else. Until Cat Mansard had come along. She had turned his safe little world upside down.

In spite of her headstrong ways, he admired Cat, and, yes, liked her a great deal. Damn it! he swore inwardly. He had to face it: he had come to love her to distraction over the past few weeks. He and Sommers had joked often enough about the nonexistent woman of perfection, and now he found himself utterly charmed by this creature of a thousand faults. And he had, in spite of the warnings of his better judgment, fantasized about a marriage to her. A marriage like those one read of in books: a marriage that did not and could not exist. He knew his mixed feelings had caused his behavior toward her to be erratic and probably confusing, but, curse it all, so had hers.

When he at last turned again to face Lady Montrose, her expression was so significant, it was as if she had been reading his mind. "I know well enough your feelings about marriage and I know as well how and why they were formed. Marriage is not for the faint of heart, Charles, but I had never before supposed that courage was lacking in you. Nevertheless, here you stand quaking before love and denying it. But ask yourself, in all honor, could you bear to see her united with someone who would crush her fine spirit? One who would marry her for reasons of estate and fortune? The question is, Charles," she said in a stern voice, "can you bear to see her marry anyone else at all?"

Had Cat known the import of Hazelforth's closely closeted interview with Lady Montrose she would indeed have felt that lady's prior encroachments on her privacy but a trifling matter. When the two emerged from the morning room some three quarters of an hour later, however, their demeanors held no suggestion of what had passed between them. Hazelforth took his leave brusquely and Lady Montrose launched into a sudden discussion of the upcoming costume ball.

"You have shown distressingly little interest in our plans, Catherine, and I am sure that poor little Cecily quite takes it to heart. She had planned, of course, for this little entertainment to divert you from your predicament."

"Oh, I am sorry, Lady Mouse. I know you both mean well. It's just that the prospect of yet another night's entertainment, another night of 'Fancy that' and 'Indeed, I'm charmed' shall surely be the death of me. I confess I had much rather spend a quiet evening with the characters of some new novel than encounter those who inhabit the mundane surroundings of the social realm."

"Why, Cat," Lady Montrose remonstrated, "surely you value at least my judgment better than that. You have not yet seen the guest list, have you? Would it pique your interest to find that not a one of them is received at Almack's? Do not look so shocked, Cat. You know these people well, although, I confess they have probably never heard of you. Indeed, you hold in your hands a novel just lately published by one of them."

"Lady Mouse! No, really?" Cat exclaimed excitedly.

"Yes, it is to be a literary and artistic evening. Out of concern for the propriety you must maintain, they shall, of course, arrive masked, but I hope the

165

evening's conversation will be diverting. Now, as for your costume . . ."

"Oh dear," Cat moaned contritely, "I have not given it a thought."

"Fortunately, I have. I have been through my trunks and found the very thing. Miss Spencer will fit it to your measurements in good time."

"Oh, do tell me what it is," Cat entreated, her enthusiasm growing now.

"That shall be a secret until next Saturday night. Just trust me that it will suit your needs quite well."

In the days that followed, Cat found her excitement about the upcoming costume ball outweighed the annoyance of the social engagements she was forced to keep each night. She had long since abandoned the notion of looking seriously for a husband at these functions and was determined to simply fulfill the letter of her grandmother's will for this Season, at any rate. Her feelings for Hazelforth continued to torment her, but at least the prospect of the costume ball afforded something pleasant upon which to focus her attention.

She now spent the greater part of each day with Cecily and Lady Montrose in preparation for the festivities. Eveline's time was much engaged with Mr. Sommers' attentions, and it was now clear, even to Cat, that he would soon make an offer. Sadly, she reflected, their newfound companionship would be at an end. Whom she would ever find to replace such an ideal companion, Cat was at a loss to tell.

Chapter Fourteen

On the morning of the costume ball, Cat awakened early to the sounds of feverish preparation. She quickly dressed and went downstairs to find the various Birdies and Mateys, as she, too, had taken to calling them, busily engaged in draping the entire downstairs with swaths of deep blue velvet.

"Beg pardon, miss," one of the footmen apologized as a heavy bolt of fabric rolled past her toes, "you'll be safer in the conservatory if you don't want to be gathered up in the drapings here."

Cat threaded her way through the bustling hallways to the conservatory where Lady Montrose and Eveline sat sipping their morning tea.

"Good morning, Cat," Lady Montrose greeted her. "Isn't this a glorious uproar? I am sorry, dear, but I have had to send Caesar and Brutus down to the kitchen. They were so downcast, poor little things — I know they'd dearly love to wreak some havoc here."

Cat assured her godmother that the kitchen would be the very place the dogs themselves would have chosen had they been capable of voicing an option.

The ladies passed the morning as quietly as they could, reading, enjoying the gardens, and attempting in general to stay out of the way as much as possible.

"I have had this idea for some time," Lady Montrose explained to them, "of creating an interior as deep and starry as the evening skies. The draperies will disguise the humdrum atmosphere of day-to-day life. And just a few candles will serve as stars. The very atmosphere for an evening of romance."

As both ladies looked rather pointedly at her, she continued hastily, "Oh, I meant romance in the sense of adventure—the literary sense, of course."

At this, Lady Montrose's butler entered. "I beg your pardon, ladies. The workmen are ready to begin on the conservatory at any time now. Would you prefer to delay them a little and have luncheon served here, or make some other arrangement?"

"No," Lady Montrose decided, "there is a great deal yet to be done. The candles, you see, Cat and Eveline, will be mounted near the ceiling to effect a starry night within the conservatory. There will be more down in the gardens and orangeries. Do you think the servants will mind if we join them downstairs today?"

"I am sure they would be delighted, your ladyship," he told her with a bow.

At this turn of events, Cat could not help but feel she had been outdone in democracy, for she had rarely visited her own kitchen since childhood; however, she and Eveline followed Lady Montrose, who had now arisen into the as yet unexplored lower regions of the house. On their arrival in the huge, airy kitchen, Cat noted that members of Lady Montrose's staff merely greeted them politely, set extra places at the table and went about their business. Her own staff surveyed her with marked surprise, which they soon suppressed, taking their cue from the natives of that domain. Caesar and Brutus, however, being true egalitarians at the heart, showed no awareness of any class differences whatever and begged morsels from whomever seemed likeliest to indulge them, regardless of their station.

Cat noted during the course of the meal that Betsy and Audrey sat at opposite ends of the long table and whenever possible darted venomous glances in the other's direction. Their animosity, however, had apparently lost its entertainment value for the rest of the staff, and she was gratified to hear Martin and Tom tell spirited accounts of their adventures in London thus far.

Martin had been several times to see the Tower of London, where an obliging Beefeater had told him horrifyingly gruesome tales of the various encounters he had had with the headless ghost of Anne Boleyn. "Often, in the dark of night, Miss Cat," he told her in hollow tones, "her spirit rises up and she walks the Bloody Tower, moaning and wailing, looking high and low for King Henry. You can see her plain as anything, they tell me. She holds her gory head up to talk to you and . . . the lips . . . move!"

Not to be outdone by this thrilling tale, Tom told about his walks through London on his half day. Not only did he believe he'd caught a glimpse of Beau Brummell, but the Prince Regent as well.

"And he hasn't stopped fiddling about with his cravat yet," Audrey snickered from her end of the table.

"Now see here, Audrey," Betsy cried. "You leave off teasing Tom. I think he looks quite nice."

"Well," Audrey minced, "I suppose you have to be satisfied with whatever you can get."

"Really, girls," Cat broke in. "We'll have none of this. You've been friends since we were all children. I want you to start acting like it."

"Sorry, Miss Cat," Betsy mumbled.

"Sorry, Miss Cat," Audrey echoed.

Neither of them looked terribly chastened, but they managed to get through the rest of the meal with a semblance of civility. As they arose, Caesar and Brutus bounded up and made as if to join them.

"Oh, dear," Cat sighed regretfully. "I'm sorry, fellows, but you'll have to stay down here today. Let's see, Martin. Can you watch them?"

Martin stood shuffling his feet, and Audrey broke in, "He's too good a boy to mention it, Miss Cat, but our Martin has his work cut out today. Errands as would break a back, eh, Martin? I'll be glad to keep an eye on them for you, though, Miss Cat. I'll keep them well out of mischief."

As Cat thanked Audrey with relief, she wondered if the girl's tendency toward idleness was not at last amending itself a little.

By late afternoon, all was in readiness for the festivities, but for the lighting of the candles. Cat's costume had arrived the day before, but Lady Montrose had been quick to take possession of it so as not to spoil the surprise. The design of Eveline's costume had also been undertaken by the little lady and the two of them controlled their curiosity with more and more difficulty as the day wore on. Finally, Lady Montrose allowed Felicia, who was nearly delirious with anticipation, to take the costumes to their chambers with instructions that she should be summoned when the two were ready.

"You go first, Eveline," Cat urged, and with a little prodding the other complied, opening her box to find a snowy white chiton, edged in gold, accompanied by a wreath of gold laurel, sandals, and a spear.

"Athena!" Cat exclaimed. "The goddess of wisdom—how appropriate!"

Eveline blushed and added, "And how comfortable for a sultry evening such as this! Lady Montrose shall have my double thanks."

Cat turned now to her own package. Inside, she found a gown made up of layers of filmy black silk whose folds sparkled as the light hit them. "What in heaven's name is this meant to be?" Cat wondered aloud.

Eveline and Felicia were at a loss, as well. "Let's see if we can tell from the accessories," Eveline suggested. From the bottom of the box, Cat pulled a pair of black velvet slippers and a parcel wrapped in tissue. Undoing it she found a curiously wrought headdress set with tiny diamonds. "Try it on, Cat!"

Cat set it on her head and the light dawned in Felicia's eyes. "How wonderful, Miss Cat!" she cried.

"Did you ever see such a thing, Miss Bartlett? Where on earth did she find such a creation?"

Cat turned to examine her image in the glass and met herself in a most surprising reflecting. "A cat!" she exclaimed. "Of course!" The headdress did indeed rise up into two peaked ears, which sparkled as she turned.

"And what is more, Miss Cat," Felicia went on as she examined her mistress, "I believe you're meant to wear your hair loose with it. What a relief!"

Eveline retired to her chamber with Felicia, who had the pleasure of arranging more docile locks than those to which she was generally accustomed while Cat set about trying on her costume. The voluminous fabric enveloped her in a gauzy cloud as she dropped the gown over her head. Contrary to current evening fashion, the sleeves fit tight to the wrist while the skirt cascaded from the bodice and fell rippling to the ground, shimmering at the slightest movement. Cat brushed her curls back and placed the headdress securely among them, then turned to look in the mirror. Cat was so entranced by what she saw there that she did not at first notice the degree to which the cut of her bodice crossed the line of decorum. As she attempted to adjust it, however, she found that matters were only made worse.

"Do stop tugging, Catherine," came Lady Montrose's voice as she entered the chamber. "The fabric is quite old. Now let me look at you. Aren't you a vision? You must forgive me for my lack of restraint, but I could not control my curiosity."

"It is lovely," Cat admitted, "but are you sure it is quite the thing. It is a bit . . ."

"Risqué?" Lady Montrose supplied. "I should hope so. Only consider whom we are entertaining tonight. I fear that they would be at least as put out by too much modesty as others might be by its want. Besides, you shall wear a domino, so what is the difference?"

"I suppose, for once, there is none. What a pleasure! Wherever did you find this?"

"Oh, I made it up from pieces. The dress was one I wore many years ago at just such an occasion. The style's been altered, but the effect is just as dashing, I must admit. The headdress was a gift from an admirer, an admiral who traveled the globe and brought me many of the treasures you see in my home."

"What became of him, Lady Mouse?"

"I lost him," she returned quietly. "Or he lost me. It doesn't really matter now. In any case, it is the current moment we must concern ourselves with, isn't it? Now how is Eveline coming?"

At that moment, Eveline crossed the threshold from her adjoining room, her diaphanous gown stirring in the breeze that came in through the open window. She, too, had gained a mysterious beauty. For a moment, the two stood regarding the transformations that had been wrought on the other's appearance. Then they both began to talk at once, each assuring the other of the suitability of their appearance, while Felicia and Lady Montrose stood by, well pleased with the work they had done that day.

Chapter Fifteen

By the time Cat and Eveline had donned the small dominoes that accompanied their costumes, irresistible strains of music could be heard drifting up the staircase. As they made their way down, they were most amused at the sight that met their eyes. Since the constraints of propriety, such as they were at Montrose House, were to be loosened still further that evening, Lady Montrose had allowed the servants access to her attics in order to deck themselves as merrily as their masters.

Martin, predictably, had dressed as a Beefeater, while Tom had decked himself out as Henry VIII, swaggering about in red velvet, brandishing a drumstick. Betsy and Audrey had been shocked into irate silence when they discovered that they had both chosen to wear the finery of Spanish dancers which, for some mysterious reason, Lady Montrose's attics held in abundance. Felicia had surprised everyone by displaying an inclination for exotic apparel and looked quite fetching, they told her, with her apron tied over her purple sari.

When the ladies finally reached the foyer, they looked about themselves, enchanted by the changes that had been wrought in so few hours. There were only a few candles lit, but their glow was supplemented by hundreds of crystal pendants suspended by wires from the ceiling. It seemed as if the entire house had indeed been transformed into a sparkling nighttime sky. Stepping dramatically from the dark recesses, their patroness presented herself. Much to their amusement, they discovered that Lady Montrose was now appareled as a brave befurred mouse as a foil to Cat's feline guise. She wore a gown of charcoal silk and her curly head was crowned by a set of little gray fur ears lined with pink velvet. Looped over her arm like a train hung a dashing gray fur tail.

"Good evening, Lady Mouse!" they greeted her, laughingly. "You look enchanting!"

"Or enchanted, perhaps," she replied in good humor, wiggling her nose at them. "Well, I must say, you both look lovelier than I had imagined. The gentlemen will have to be stouthearted indeed to withstand you for long tonight. I vow, nothing shall astonish me this evening!"

As Cat looked about, she was surprised to see the tables laden with a feast for far more than the number of guests warranted. Noticing her attention, Lady Montrose explained that she not only disapproved of the paltry refreshments served at most gatherings, but also confided that many of her guests tonight could very well use a good meal, the arts being a less lucrative pursuit than many.

"It is also nice to be able to encourage them to

drink their fill of champagne without fearing too great a lack of sobriety an empty stomach might occasion," she went on, then suddenly stopped herself, for Cat had turned quite red. "I am sorry, my dear! I hadn't meant to . . ."

"Please don't worry," Cat reassured her hastily. "It is nice to be assured that I, too, can indulge myself with less apprehension than I might otherwise have, for indeed I have every intention of having a sip or two."

As it was a costume ball, Lady Montrose had determined that her guests would be announced according to the character whom they portrayed. Thus it was that such interesting pairings as Geoffrey Chaucer and Cleopatra, Prester John and Marie de France found themselves at home in the company of their hostesses, Mistress Cat and Lady Mouse, and the guests of honor, Bo Peep and a very sheepish Little Boy Blue, known in more mundane surroundings as Cecily and John.

As Cat circulated among the guests, taking care to sample the buffet as she sipped her champagne, she was fascinated to overhear variant phrasings of sonnets hotly debated, rumors of Byron's philanderings discussed, and a scene for a new Gothic novel plotted out. She was somewhat downcast as she realized that even all her years of reading had not prepared her to enter the conversation; she could but marvel at the breadth of knowledge, particularly that of women, displayed so brilliantly therein. She determined to widen her circle of acquaintances to include them should her fortunes allow her to do so.

Although Mr. Sommers, fortuitously garbed as Plato and looking wise indeed, had been among the first to arrive, Cat had been unable to identify Mr. Hazelforth among the crowd. Indeed she had been quite curious to discover what costume he had chosen for the evening's festivities; she had, she now realized, merely assumed that he would be there. It was more than likely, she admitted with a disappointed pang, that entertainments such as these did not tempt him.

As Cat threaded her way among the guests, she was much surprised to find herself approached by Mr. Sommers, who self-consciously requested the privilege of a private interview. Her curiosity running at a high pitch, she led him through the merrymakers (and through several yards of blue velvet swathing) to a little drawing room. There, she was much diverted to observe this generally contained gentleman pace about some minutes in wretched consternation, mindless of the singular picture he made in his toga and sandals.

"Miss Catherine, I do not, I confess, know quite how to begin . . ." he faltered.

"Yet I am sure you will give it a valiant effort," she prompted with a smile, as she seated herself primly and waited patiently. Indeed, it was all she could do to disguise her amusement as poor Mr. Sommers recommenced his agitated promenade.

"You see," he began again, adjusting his golden laurel wreath which had slipped down over one eye. "I . . . It's Miss Bartlett!"

177

"Yes? Miss Bartlett?" she queried in maddeningly innocent tones.

"Well, you see . . . I mean to make an offer. That is, I mean to propose marriage to her tonight," he finally succeeded in articulating.

Although Cat had suspected that this announcement was indeed the purpose of this odd conference, it was with mixed feelings that she at last heard his intentions pronounced. "I wish you joy, of course, Mr. Sommers, but this is a turn around indeed. I had thought you were determined to remain single."

"I had always thought so," he admitted with a frown, "until I met Eveline. Er, Miss Bartlett."

In spite of her affection for the man, Cat could not help toying with him just a little. "And why do you wish to speak with me?" she asked ingenuously.

"Well, Miss Catherine," he said with some consternation, "it is a matter of correctness. It is customary, as you know, to obtain permission from someone in order to pay one's addresses."

"Yes, and Miss Bartlett has no relations. I understand that much."

"Well, Miss Bartlett is your, er, companion, so you are by way of being her employer and . . ." he continued wretchedly. "Please, Miss Catherine. You must have pity on me here. I know this is an odd situation for me, a man some years your senior, to be making such an application, but I thought it best."

At this, Cat finally gave in to the comedy of the situation and laughed merrily. "Mr. Sommers, indeed I pray you do not agitate yourself so distressingly. Eveline is my friend and companion, but, as far as I am concerned, she is also the mistress of her fate. I wish her to be happy, that is all. If accepting your offer will make her so, then it has my blessing."

At that, Mr. Sommers shook her hand warmly, and adjusting his troublesome wreath once more, he went off in search of his chosen one, leaving Cat to ponder ruefully her own belabored heart as she returned to her guests. If only she were able to turn back time, she told herself with a rueful sigh, she would have taken more pains not to fall in love. It didn't matter that the crowd scintillated about her, that candles glowed, that champagne sparkled. It was a very odd phenomenon, but nothing mattered at all for a heart whose love was not returned.

During the course of the evening, Cat found herself approached by an excited Cecily. "Oh, Cat, do come here and look at Miss Bartlett and Mr. Sommers! I am sure something is afoot."

Before Cecily could lead Cat in their direction, they were themselves approached by the happy pair in their matching classical apparel. As they drew near, Mr. Sommers whispered something to Eveline, drew her hand to his lips, and retreated into the crowd.

"Oh, Cat, Cecily!" Eveline cried. "I cannot tell you how happy I am! Mr. Sommers, Richard, has asked me to marry him. Without fortune. Without connections. Can you imagine!? He loves me!"

As her former pupils wished her joy and assured her that they could well imagine such a wonder, Eveline went on, "He's gone to find Hazelforth, if he's here yet, and break the news to him. I suppose he's

179

half afraid to do so, they've both been so dedicated to their single status for so long. Well, now, I am afraid poor Hazelforth will have to go it alone."

At this remark, Cat could but sigh inwardly. As Eveline left them in order to share her news with Lady Montrose, Cecily patted her comfortingly on the shoulder. "Well, Cat, you shall just have to come and spend the winter with me and John. It will be far too solitary for you at Sparrowell, and besides, I'm certain that Mr. Hazelforth will visit us as well, and the two of you can lay your plans for next year's Season. I'm sure you both . . ."

But here Cat surprised her cousin by draining the glass of champagne she held, taking yet another from a passing tray, and proceeding through the assemblage into the garden, abruptly leaving Cecily in midsentence. When John joined his wife some moments later, she was still smiling smugly to herself, well content to sit back and observe the evening's developments.

Cat made her way through the conservatory and out into the refreshing night air, and stood looking down into the candle-lit gardens. There, she was surprised to see her Mr. Hazelforth sitting quite alone in the orangeries. She regarded him with a mix of emotions. Watching unobserved for a moment, she debated whether it was wisdom or folly that prompted her to go to him and further torment her heart. However, she decided finally, he looked quite lonely sitting there, so isolated from the festivities. He, too, has been deserted this evening by his best friend, she told herself. She quickly appropriated another glass of champagne and advanced down the staircase toward him. The air was pungent with the spicy scent of summer's blossoms, and in the light of a dozen flickering candles, Cat could see that he smiled at her approach.

"I was not aware you had arrived, Mr. Hazelforth. You did not choose to wear a costume this evening?" she ventured as she held out the glass to him.

"No," he returned with a short laugh, as he took the champagne from her. He stood a moment looking at her. The shifting gossamer of her costume fluttered in the slight breeze, reflecting the light of the candles about them. The diamonds in her headdress, too, picked up the glimmer with every motion. He was glad, though, that she wore the domino, for he did not know if he was equal to encountering her gaze unmasked tonight. "Like you, Mistress Cat, I have decided it is best to forego disguise and come as myself. But what brings you down into the garden? Why have you left the festivities? I should have thought these revels would be diverting indeed to one of your turn of mind and interests. Yet here you stand, the corners of your mouth turned down, sighing into the night. Come now. Why so sad, my little Cat?"

"Then you have not heard?" she replied, straining for control. The candlelight plays tricks, she reminded herself; it only seems that he looks at me so softly. "I have spoken to Mr. Sommers. We are both to be deprived of our companions."

"So, Sommers has made his move, has he? The charming Miss Bartlett has won him at last. Well, I wish them joy," he said, draining his glass and setting it down. "He is a braver man than I."

"I should not think that marriage would be such an intimidating prospect where there is love," she countered, her voice shaking just a little with emotion. This would never do, she told herself angrily. He must not suspect how she felt. Mastering herself, she went on in a more placid tone, "But perhaps your loss will not be so hard on you, Mr. Hazelforth. I shall miss Eveline, however, and I do not at all look forward to a winter of solitude."

"Nor do I," he agreed. They stood together in silence for a time, listening to the distant melody of the orchestra, and each wishing desperately that they might divine the thoughts of the other. The candles wavered in the breeze, and Cat sighed, her throat tightening.

Finally, Hazelforth took a deep breath, squared his shoulders, and took her by the hand. "Come here, Cat. Stand where I can see you. Take off that wretched domino. That's much better. You are especially beautiful tonight, you know. But then you are always beautiful."

Dazed, Cat looked up at him in the candlelight. His eyes were dark with emotion. "I remember the day I first saw you, there in the sacristy," he went on, his voice coming softly to her through the semi-darkness. "Not only beautiful, but so very much yourself, so very different from anyone I had ever met before. In spite of your tempers, in spite of the fact that you could barely tolerate my presence — yes, I knew it well — I was compelled to seek you out. I could not help myself then. Nor can I now."

Cat had little time to reflect on this declaration, for she almost immediately found herself enveloped in Hazelforth's arms as his lips urgently sought hers. She wondered for a fleeting second why she had no inclination at all to struggle in this embrace, and then lost track of everything except her rushing senses. For what seemed an eternity, she was only aware of his warm lips on hers. Then, his kisses and her own grew deeper, more impatient. As she caught her breath, his mouth traveled from her own, down her neck to her tangled locks and onto her bare shoulders, sending small shivers up and down her spine as he pressed her to him urgently. Breathlessly, relentlessly, he continued in his downward progression, until at last she felt his lips reach the valley between her breasts and linger there as his hands buried themselves in her hair. She drew in her breath sharply, and involuntarily her champagne glass slipped from her hand, shattering on the stones at her feet.

At that instant, Hazelforth released her suddenly, muttering a low curse in the darkness. "What have I done, Cat?" he whispered in anguish. "I am no better than . . ."

"Please, Mr. Hazelforth . . . I beg you not to . . ." she hesitated, her voice faint. She did not, she realized with a guilty flush, wish for him to stop at all, yet she could hardly entreat him to proceed. She put her hands up to her cheeks, uncertain how to continue.

He stood a few moments in wretched silence, feeling a cad and a fool. Here stood his love, trembling before him, unable to meet his eye. How could he have acted thus, particularly after his condemnation of Abelwhite? And how could he explain to Cat that, in spite of his actions, he did love and respect her? He waited until he had recovered himself before he spoke to her again. "Forgive me, Miss Catherine. Believe me that I had no intention of . . . You may trust that I shall call early tomorrow to make my addresses. Let me go now to ask permission of Lady Montrose." He took her hand and pressed it, then disappeared into the darkness, leaving Cat's head and heart spinning.

If Cat had felt any momentary joy in hearing Hazelforth's intentions, it soon faded as reason reined in her heart. True, he had said he intended to make his addresses, to propose marriage, but his voice had been more anguished than impassioned. Worse, he had spoken not a single word of love. Would he make such a commitment simply because he felt he had compromised her? Merely in order to separate himself from the Henry Abelwhites of the world? Perhaps, she thought, perhaps. Marriage was what she had wanted, she finally admitted, but marriage with love.

It was not impossible, though. I can make him love me, she insisted stubbornly to herself. However, a small voice from within whispered with cold persistence, might not a man such as Hazelforth eventually resent his situation? Might not his regard change slowly to bitterness and thence to hatred? The candles about her began to sputter, their dying light mocking her. With a heavy heart, she made her decision. In the morning she would offer to release Hazelforth from his pledge. Perhaps, she thought with some small hope, he would decline.

Cat's sorrowful meditation was interrupted as she heard the sounds of the guests beginning to make their departures, and she turned slowly toward the house to help Lady Montrose bid them a good night. When she reached the foyer, she saw that her godmother and Mr. Hazelforth stood there side by side. While Lady Montrose smiled knowingly at her, she saw to her despair that Hazelforth's face had not lost its stricken look. He joined her and whispered hollowly, "It has all been arranged. I shall come by in the morning as early as is proper. Good night, Catherine." At this he pressed her hand uncertainly once more and left her to the chatter of the departing guests.

When the last of the company had finally been seen off, Cat was distressed to recognize the signs of weariness beneath Lady Montrose's smiling face. As Cat helped her make her way up the stairs, Lady Montrose turned to her and said, "I am very happy for you indeed, Cat. Many years ago I loved a man and lost him. I am glad that you have not been so careless with your love as I was with mine."

Cat found she could make no rejoinder, but silently accompanied the little lady to her apartments, where she bid her a good night. Turning down the hall to her own chamber, she stopped a moment to regard her image in a tall mirror one last time, reflecting that in it she had experienced both the heights and depths of emotion in the space of a half hour.

Just as she reached her chamber, however, she heard her name called out and found herself accosted by Audrey, obviously distraught. "Oh, Miss Cat," she wailed, wringing her hands. "It's them dogs of yours! They've gone and run away!"

"When was this, Audrey?" Cat asked in sudden concern. "How long have they been gone?"

"Just now, just this very minute. They was out the kitchen door after a stray cat, fast as two greased pigs." Here, Audrey succumbed to noisy tears accompanied by a distressingly nasal whine, her small eyes puffed and pitifully red.

"Well, don't worry, Audrey," Cat reassured her. "They won't have strayed far from the kitchens if I know them. I'll just go down and call to them."

"Oh, yes, please do, Miss Cat!" Audrey exclaimed looking relieved. "That would do the trick right enough, never a doubt at all."

As they made their way down the staircase together, they encountered Eveline, smiling dreamily, on her way up. "I won't be too long, Eveline. Go on to bed. It seems Caesar and Brutus are up to their old tricks. They've played poor Audrey false and run away."

"Are you sure you don't need me, Cat?" Eveline asked. "They can be quite difficult to catch."

"Oh, no, Miss Bartlett," Audrey broke in quickly. "I'm sure when they hear Miss Cat's voice they'll come a-running."

Cat was a little surprised when Audrey led her down through the orangeries to the end of the garden rather than toward the park. "You're sure this is the way they went?" she asked.

"Oh, yes, Miss Cat, I'm certain sure. Why, is that the little fellows down there?" she asked, holding aloft her lantern and taking a few tentative steps into the impenetrable darkness.

"I don't see them, Audrey. Caesar?" Cat called doubtfully, stepping into the dim alley. "Brutus?" She took another step and suddenly felt herself seized roughly from behind as a hand forced a cloth soaked in some pungent concoction over her face. She struggled for a moment, then lost consciousness as darkness closed in from all directions.

Chapter Sixteen

Several times during the night, Cat regained her consciousness enough to realize that she was confined in a carriage and being conveyed at a great speed, without apparent attention to either safety or comfort. Since the drug was reapplied forcefully each time she so much as groaned, Cat attempted to be still and feign unconsciousness. If she could rest and bide her time, she hoped she might be in possession of her wits should an opportunity for escape arise. Through her fogged senses she could hear snatches of a conversation, the voices of a man and a woman. Audrey? But who else? Surely it could not be Mr. D'Ashley? Could he have been so competent? It did not seem at all likely, yet all evidence pointed to a plot between the pair. She also wondered with increasing alarm whether her little dogs had indeed shared some part of her fate, or were fast asleep on her eiderdown pillows.

The carriage stopped once, about dawn, for a change of horses, then proceeded on its rattling way. Cat could have cried with discomfort, so cramped and bruised was she, as well as nauseous from whatever they had used to subdue her senses. Wisely, however, she did her best to sleep and conserve her strength for the trials that undoubtedly lay ahead.

Hazelforth had spent a restless night, fraught with self-recrimination at his excesses of the night before. He had cursed himself roundly for his lack of control and wondered if he could ever forgive himself the look of dismay that had suffused Cat's features on the previous evening. He felt like a hypocrite, having soundly trounced and transported that cad, Abelwhite, but a few weeks earlier. Now he stood convicted in his own mind of a similar, if not worse, offense. As he tossed and turned, he vowed he would make it up to her. He had waged his internal battle long enough; at last he had reconciled himself to the fact that he loved her and had finally made that plain to her. Or had he? He hadn't quite been able to pronounce the words, had he? It was this realization that sent him early from his lodgings to pace about in the park in front of Montrose House. He would set that last matter straight, should there be any doubt, as speedily as possible.

He had hardly arrived, however, when he was met with the extraordinary sight of both Miss Bartlett and Lady Montrose, still in their wrappers, stepping out the front door of Montrose House and sending several footmen running speedily in several directions. At the same time, Martin, the boy of all work, came tearing through the park within a few feet of Hazelforth.

"Ho there, Martin!" he called out, catching the boy by the arm. "Why all the uproar?"

"Mr. Hazelforth! What good luck! I was just sent to fetch you and Mr. Sommers. It's our Miss Cat! She's gone!"

"What do you mean, boy?" he cried impatiently.

"When Felicia went up to take Miss Cat her chocolate this morning, she wasn't there. And her bed hadn't been slept in all night neither. And the dogs! Caesar and Brutus are gone, too!"

At this disclosure, Hazelforth felt himself stricken to the core. Cat had run away into the night. Had his attentions, then, been so unwelcome?

"I'd best be off to find Mr. Sommers now," Martin continued breathlessly, and was soon dashing across the green. Wretched with self-recrimination and worry, Hazelforth made his way quickly to Montrose House and joined the distraught ladies just inside the door.

"Martin has just told me that Cat and her dogs are gone," he told them hurriedly. "Quickly! What else do you know? Did she leave a note?"

"A note?" Lady Montrose protested in some confusion. "There could be no note. Why, Hazelforth, she has most certainly been abducted."

"And it's that horrid Mr. D'Ashley, I am almost certain of it," Eveline cried miserably. "We should have listened to you and Mr. Sommers!"

By the time Eveline had explained that not only had Audrey been missing that morning, but related what was known about her relationship with the said Mr. D'Ashley, Hazelforth was convinced as well, relieved on one score, but desperate with alarm on all others. Just then, Felicia bustled into the foyer dragging along with her Tom, the footman, who had clearly not been long roused from his bed. "Oh, Mr. Hazelforth, thank the good Lord you're here. Just listen to what Tom has to say about all this," she cried urgently. "Go on now, Tom."

"Well, Mr. Hazelforth," he began with slow deliberation, "it's like this. Just the other day, Wednesday it was, I happened to be out and about the town when I caught sight of that Mr. D'Ashley fellow. Well, he's a suspicious character, let me tell you. All havey-cavey, I thought from the very first, so I took it on myself to follow about after him on the sly."

If truth were known, Tom had indeed followed Mr. D'Ashley about that day, but for the sole purpose of observing his progress from tailor to snuff shop to haberdasher. Tom, who was convinced he had an eye for fashion, was far more taken with that gentleman's dandyish apparel than he would care to admit.

"Get on with it, Tom," Felicia prodded, delivering an impatient little dig in the poor footman's ribs.

"Well, as I was about to say," he continued huffily, "it wasn't too terrible long before I seen this Mr. D'Ashley meet a gentleman, by arrangement like. A very *familiar* gentleman, mind you."

"Out with it, man!" cried Hazelforth impatiently.

"Well," Tom pronounced self-importantly, looking about at the rapt faces of his audience, "it was none other than our Mr. Snagworth of Sparrowell Hall!"

"Snagworth!" cried Eveline.

"The very one," Tom concurred with a significant nod.

"Fetch me a horse," Hazelforth commanded.

Sleep had, at last, overcome Cat for several hours. When the carriage finally did come to a halt, it was beginning to grow dark once again, and Cat, though still feigning unconsciousness, was considerably more clearheaded than she had been earlier and surmised that the effects of the drug had worn off. When Mr. D'Ashley now attempted to rouse her from her supposed stupor, she perversely remained limp, and noted with a good deal of satisfaction that the villain was forced to grunt and strain as he awkwardly attempted to remove her (and the accompanying fifteen or twenty yards of shifting fabric of her costume) from the carriage. He succeeded at last, however, and tossed her unceremoniously over his shoulder like a sack of grain.

"Zounds, Jeff, you haven't kilt her have you?" came a familiar voice through the darkness. Could it possibly be Snagworth? One swift glance beneath her lowered lids confirmed her conjecture. In light of past behavior, his complicity, at least, did not surprise Cat, although the vindication of her earlier suspicions was hardly rewarding at this point. She did wonder, however, how he came to know Mr. D'Ashley. This she soon discovered.

"Never fear, Uncle," returned her captor with a grunt as he shifted her weight, "she'll sleep it off before long."

"Who's this other one?" Snagworth asked testily, jerking his head at the white-faced parlor maid.

"Ah, yes, Audrey. My artful accomplice. You must remember my uncle, Mr. Snagworth."

"Mr. Snagworth? Your uncle? Why, Jeff, you've not been straight with me, and that's a fact!" came Audrey's querulous voice. "Why, you told me you was a lord's son, disinherited though you was, and I'm for certain sure our Mr. Snagworth here ain't got no ounce of noble blood in him."

"Shut her up or make her useful, Jeff," Snagworth snarled. "Now where's them dogs?"

"Up there." Peeking again through partially closed eyes, Cat could see Snagworth remove a basket, intricately secured with all manner of ropes and twine, from the top of the carriage. "Careful of those boys, Uncle. They've got a set of vicious teeth on them."

"I know all about them devils, Jeff. It'll be a pleasure to take off an ear or two should we need to make our guest a little more open to our schemes."

"Oh, Jeff," wailed Audrey, who had grown quite attached to the little dogs in spite of their naughtiness, "you never said nothing about that."

"Quiet," he snarled at her, and she began to weep noisily. Cat, whose apprehensions were now even more severe, felt herself being conveyed into a building. From her vantage point she could see only the carpet and lower portions of the furnishings, but she soon realized with a mixture of relief and outrage that she had been brought home once again to her beloved Sparrowell Hall.

"Where shall I put her down, Uncle?" D'Ashley called out indistinctly, for a good deal of the slippery fabric of Cat's gown had by now bunched itself up in front of his mouth.

"Lock her and them hateful dogs in the library. We've got some talking to do, boy. Can this one watch her?" Snagworth asked in disparaging tones.

"Audrey will do anything I ask her, won't you, love?" D'Ashley returned with an insinuating laugh. "Don't worry, Uncle.

Soon Cat heard the doors to the library open and suppressed a groan as she was dumped heavily onto a leather sofa.

"Here now, Audrey," came D'Ashley's voice, "you keep good watch on her. Now, hold on to this

194

musket. If she tries anything, fire it up into the ceiling."

Audrey took the musket with quaking hands as the men made their way out. As soon as the key could be heard in the door, however, Audrey placed the musket on the table beside her and wiped her hands anxiously on her skirts. Then she knelt down by the basket.

"Are you all right, boys?" Audrey whispered uncertainly. "You know I'd set you free if I could, but if they ever found me out, they'd have my head on a platter and no mistake." She patted the basket apprehensively and made some comforting noises before dissolving once again into extravagant weeping.

Cat lay still, thinking for some time. It was clear that she was in some danger. Moreover, the likelihood of her abduction having been discovered early on was quite likely exceedingly remote, as was the possibility that anyone would fathom the destination of her captors. It was also true that neither Snagworth nor his nephew had taken any trouble to lower their voices so, except for the conspirators, she realized she must be quite alone in the house. In short, a rescue was not to be looked for any time soon. That task, Cat determined with a sinking feeling, would have to be undertaken by herself before any harm could come either to herself or Caesar and Brutus.

She realized immediately that several aspects of the situation were in her favor, however, not the least of which was that the men had apparently underestimated their victim and overestimated themselves and Audrey. In addition, Cat not only knew her own home far more intimately than they, but she had also spent much of the day sleeping and was as well-rested as they were fatigued. It would just be a matter of time before Audrey, whose emotions were by now quite spent, fell prey to her exhaustion.

In this hope, Cat was not disappointed. Before half an hour had passed, the sounds of Audrey's sobbing had been transformed to whimpering and thence to muffled snores. After several minutes had passed thus, Cat was convinced that she must seize on this opportunity to put her hastily formulated plan into action.

Snagworth and his nephew could not have chosen a room more suited to Cat's purposes than the library. She rose quietly from the sofa and moved silently toward the massive fireplace. The priest's hole and the passages which connected it to the rest of the house had been a part of the original design of the house some three hundred years earlier. Although these clandestine features had been put to but little use during those troubled times, they had provided an endless source of amusement (and mischief) for the children of ensuing generations.

Cat and Cecily had known those passages well, and it was with a practiced hand that Cat twisted one carved rosette below the mantel, and a panel at her side swung wide. As was the custom of the house, candles and a phosphorous box were situated just inside. Her escape route now secured, she picked up the musket and the still-bound basket in which Caesar and Brutus had been incarcerated, entered the passage and swung the door shut behind her. It was fortunate, she reflected, that she knew these passages well enough to forego the use of a candle. The basket and musket were a heavier, more awkward load than she had anticipated, and she did not think she could have carried one more thing.

As she slowly made her way through the darkness, she continued to sort her thoughts. Part of Cat's dilemma as she considered her predicament had been her dogs. Where could she put them where they would be quiet and out of harm's way? She could, of course, leave them for a time in the passageway, but should they happen to bark and be overheard, her plans would be thwarted. As it turned out, the solution occurred to her as she remembered their history of bad behavior. The pantry, she decided, must be the very place for them, for nothing would distract them from laying waste to its tempting contents were they given free rein, and surely they would simply go to sleep once they had eaten their fill.

Cat cautiously followed the passage downward until she reached the kitchen level. Resting her load on one hip, she was able to free a hand. Slowly, she slid a slot backward to peek at the room before entering. All was dark. She cautiously engaged the lever which shifted back an apparently stationary cupboard to form an entry to the room. Setting down her burden with relief, she found a lamp and lit it, crossed to the pantry and opened the door. There she saw several meat pies, rounds of cheese, and some fresh custard creams. Surely this repast would keep the little gluttons sufficiently engaged while she went about her business.

Swiftly, she set about freeing the basket from its bonds; indeed Mr. D'Ashley must have been in mortal dread of the little dogs for she eventually was forced to resort to the use of a stout kitchen knife to complete this task. When she finally opened the basket, the sight that met her eyes prompted a most unladylike oath, for not only had the dogs been confined within the basket, but their muzzles and paws had been bound as well. Only fury restrained the tears which Cat felt pricking at her eyes. Snagworth and D'Ashley would pay dearly for this, she vowed, as she set the little fellows free, fetched water, and tried to reassure them. She was much heartened to see that the pair responded with resilience, particularly when they happened to spot the proximity of the meat pies, and with some measure of assurance she reviewed the rest of her plan.

Chapter Seventeen

Hazelforth had no real assurance that following the road to Sparrowell Hall would afford him anything other than the opportunity to interrogate Snagworth. Whether or not he would find any sign of Cat was another question altogether; nevertheless, the need to take action, to follow some lead, however remote, spurred him desperately on. The Bow Street Runners had been summoned, of course, but to have sat about and waited for their investigation to yield information would have been intolerable for him.

He had taken care as he progressed along the road to question travelers, innkeepers, and various others he met about any encounters they might have had with a party which seemed excessively pressed or secretive. Several thought that they had perhaps heard a coach rattle by at some speed during the night, while others vowed they had heard nothing. At one inn, however, the proprietor admitted that just such a coach had passed through, changed horses and gone on its way.

None of the occupants had descended. There was nothing remarkable about it, the man professed as he spit into the dust, except for the paltry tip. Besides, the light had been quite dim and he doubted he would be able to recognize the driver again in any case.

This information, while fragmentary and conveyed with an expression of rude boredom, was enough to give Hazelforth a new burst of energy. Quickly changing horses, he sped on down the highway, endeavoring to keep a rein on his imagination, which minute by minute painted more and more dire scenes of Cat's distress. Again and again he cursed himself for having done so little to protect her. He should have investigated this D'Ashley. He had had misgivings and ignored them. It was inexcusable, he berated himself. Criminally stupid. As the miles passed beneath him, however, he was at least heartened at the knowledge that one man traveling on horseback had a fair chance of overtaking a carriage, even if it had the benefit of a sizable headstart.

He had not gone much further when he encountered another horseman, similarly intent, proceeding toward him from the opposite direction. As soon as the features of the other were clear, each brought his mount to an abrupt and dusty halt.

"Mr. Hazelforth!" the rider called out as he reined in.

"Chumley!" he returned in surprise, for it was

indeed the butler of Sparrowell Hall. "Quickly! Tell me what brings you this way?"

"I've come to warn Miss Cat," he panted breathlessly. "There's something ill afoot at Sparrowell. These last weeks, I've been watching Mr. Snagworth rummaging around in the papers, receiving mysterious callers, digging up the rose garden. And when Mr. Bagsmith calls, he keeps a close watch on him and won't leave him alone for a minute with any of the staff. Now he's told us all to take a little holiday—all but turned us out, that is. There are those that took advantage of it quickly enough, but some of us have our suspicions."

At this disclosure, Hazelforth quickly revealed the events that had taken place in the last few hours. Without another word, Chumley turned his horse about and the two set forth together toward Sparrowell.

Just as Cat was about to leave the pantry, she heard the voices of Snagworth and his nephew approaching the kitchen, and her heart seemed to stand still for an instant. It was well, she reflected after a moment, that Caesar and Brutus were too quietly and steadily intent upon their dinners to sound their yapping alarm, for she was not quite ready for an encounter. Quickly extinguishing her lamp, she stepped back into the shadows as the wavering glimmer of their light approached, and she strained to hear what passed between the conspirators.

"Well, Jeff," came Snagworth's aggrieved voice, "you've botched things right enough now. Beefwit! You was supposed to charm the chit, make her fall in love with you, elope with her. Then we'd have had twenty years to find that treasure. I've dreamed of that treasure since I first heard of it two years ago when I come here. But, no. Not only do I have to make a damned fool of myself playing the highwayman so you can be the gallant, but then come to find it's all been for naught."

"Well, Uncle," D'Ashley sneered, his voice dripping with sarcasm, "if you'd been a halfway creditable highwayman, I could have passed the whole thing off. But up I ride just like we planned, all ready to rescue the damsel in distress, only to find you put to rout by the creature. You know I only agreed to this knot-headed scheme because you told me she was a sweet, biddable thing. A regular Bath miss you told me. Instead, I find a tyrant ordering everybody about like an overseer. No, I tell you, Uncle, I pity the poor man that ends up with that Tartar. Not only that, but I get myself injured into the bargain. I warrant this poor ankle will never be right again."

Unmoved by his nephew's catalogue of sorrows, Snagworth continued to fume. "Only look how I've wasted my hard-earned money getting an education for you so's you could talk right and all.

Then what do you do, I ask you? Ignore the lady and saddle yourself with a kitchen maid. So here we sit," he snorted in disgust, "with a kidnapped heiress — a hanging offense mind you — and no closer to that treasure than a poxy beggar to the queen's chamber. And just what do you propose we do?"

"It's simple," D'Ashley snorted. "We just force her to tell us where the treasure's hid."

"Just force her, he says!" Snagworth squealed, tearing at his hair. "You've said yourself a hundred times she's as vile-tempered as an ogress!"

"You forget, Uncle, we've got those scurvy dogs hostage, and she thinks more of them than most people do of their own children. Mark me, all we need do is tickle them with a knife and she'll tell us anything we want to know. What's more, I don't have to spend the rest of my life leg-shackled to her. And after we find that treasure, we just ride ourselves down to the harbor, get on a boat — yes, I've checked, there's one bound for Barbados — and we live like kings forever."

As Snagworth scratched his chin and pondered this scenario, Cat, too, was deep in thought as the small mysteries which had nagged at her fell into place. If she had known the legend of Sparrowell's treasure would ever bring about such difficulties, she'd have posted a notice explaining the particulars long ago. Moreover, young D'Ashley's comments as to her suitability as a wife reminded her all too intensely of poor Mr. Hazelforth. If any good could come of her predicament, it was that that gentleman's noble plans had been interrupted. Hearing herself described so candidly was humiliating, but effective. More than ever, she was determined to release him from his promise, for she loved him far too much to burden him with her shrewish nature.

"Now, Uncle," D'Ashley went on, "you sent me the all-clear signal two days ago — how long have we got to find the treasure?"

"Till midday tomorrow at least. I sent the servants off yesterday — what a charitable and harmless old fool they think me for such a holiday. That fellow Bagsmith came by four days ago, so he won't be back for at least another month."

"That settles it," his nephew concluded. "We'll have to look sharp, though. I want this beastly business over and done with and ourselves well on our way to sunnier climes before anyone's the wiser. Let's go and wake her up and have it out."

"What about that other one, that Audrey?" his uncle asked suspiciously. "What's to be done with her?"

"Her usefulness is just about done. That ugly baggage fancies I'll marry her," he snickered cruelly, "but maybe there's a chore or two for her to take care of before I leave her weeping at the dock."

On hearing this conversation, Cat determined that she, too, would do well to act quickly, for aside from the musket she held gingerly in both hands, surprise was her best weapon. She had been watching through a crack in the pantry door and as they rose and turned to go upstairs once again, she stepped from her hiding place.

"Wait just a moment, if you please, gentlemen," she requested with apparent composure in spite of her quaking heart. Advancing a bit further into the room, she leveled the musket at them. Had Cat felt the inclination to laugh at such a juncture, the faces she now met would have provided an admirable diversion, their eyes almost starting from their heads with incredulity and anger. "I believe, sirs, that I shall be forced to put an end to your very interesting plans."

"Botched it again!" hissed Snagworth, his face crimson with wrath. "You worthless runt! Good for nothing ninnyhammer! I always knew I should have drownded you when you was a baby!"

"Muzzle yourself, Uncle," the other snapped in equally foul humor, "and let me handle this or we shall both swing. Well, Miss Catherine," D'Ashley went on with seeming ease, "I see that useless Audrey has fallen down on the job. I suppose I shouldn't be surprised. But you don't really imagine I would have left her alone with a loaded musket, do you? She'd have blown her own foot off before too long. Now just give that musket to me and sit down here nicely. Just do as we say and no harm will come to you."

Cat did not know whether to believe D'Ashley or not, for indeed she had not thought to check the musket and dared not look down to do so now. As she stood frozen, weighing the consequences of possible actions, D'Ashley began to approach her cautiously, one slow step after the other. Well, she thought to herself, if this musket is so harmless, why does the villain approach so warily? Experimentally, she raised the weapon and put her thumb to the trigger. D'Ashley froze. Cat smiled.

"Now do step back, Mr. D'Ashley — or whatever it is you are really called." Cat advanced some paces further into the room as the two conspirators, their brows now beaded with nervous perspiration, retreated hastily before her. "Now, we shall have to see that the two of you are made harmless. Just how shall we do that, I wonder? Sit down at the table and let me think for just a moment."

Just then, a noise issued from the direction of the pantry and Cat's split second of inattention was all D'Ashley needed to make a lunge for the musket. He flung himself forward, grabbing her arm and pointing the weapon away from himself. It discharged at once with a deafening crack. As Cat struggled to regain control of the weapon, it went off once again. This time its thunderous report was combined with the piercing cries of Mr. Snagworth, who had sought refuge under the table at the sound of the first report.

"Oh, I am killed!" he cried out in anguish. "A sorry end to a sorrier life."

As the wound, which was indeed quite insignificant, appeared to be restricted to Snagworth's posterior region, Cat felt but little apprehension for his well-being. D'Ashley, however, had sprung away when the musket had discharged its second load and she now faced him holding only the useless weapon in her hand. She considered momentarily that she might attempt to beat him about the head with it, but she doubted she could muster that sort of brutality.

Cat felt in desperate straits indeed just then, her heart pounding. Without a weapon, she could not conceive how she might contrive an escape, even in light of Snagworth's wound and D'Ashley's incompetence. Soon enough, she would surely be overpowered and forced to who knew what ends? If only she could put her hands to a knife or cleaver, the match might be made more equal. Already she could see D'Ashley's eyes casting furtively about for just such a weapon. As his gaze returned to her, he seemed to be evaluating her capacity to flee him in the restrictive yardage of the costume she still wore. It was, therefore, with a good deal of surprise and relief that Cat observed Mr. D'Ashley's expression change to one of horror. Growing gray in the face, he backed away from her in untainted terror.

"Keep them away from me!" he screamed shrilly, jumping up onto the kitchen table. "I'll do anything! Just keep them back!"

In utter confusion, Cat had not the least idea

what to make of this sudden and inexplicable change in D'Ashley's demeanor. When she discovered the source of his panic, however, it took all the self-control she could command to refrain from laughing out loud, for advancing stiff-legged and growling viciously came Caesar and Brutus, their beards and mouths quite covered with custard and cream.

"Keep the rabid beasts off!" D'Ashley cried, beside himself. "Don't let them bite me! I'll do anything you want!"

"Lord help us," Snagworth chimed in tearfully. "First to be shot to death in the arse, then to perish of the rabies! It's all your fault, you witless cawker!"

D'Ashley could but quake by way of reply, for, quite understandably, the much-abused dogs had taken him in even keener dislike in the hours since their ordeal began. They stood bristling and snarling before him, their eyes glowing almost red. Now, with the wrathful pair holding her assailants at bay, Cat was able to search about the kitchen, fetch a knife and a length of stout rope with which to bind them.

"I promise I shall keep them back, Mr. D'Ashley," she promised, "but you shall have to bind your uncle. I doubt he's in any sort of danger, for I see the musket ball is lodged in the table leg. It must only have scratched him a little."

D'Ashley stared at her speechlessly for a moment so that Cat was forced to brandish the blade before him in what she hoped was a menacing manner. It clearly served her purpose that he already thought her such a monster that he considered her capable of anything. Without further ado, he picked up the rope she had tossed him. Although Snagworth winced and groaned and vowed it felt more like a mortal wound, D'Ashley wasted no time in complying with Cat's request, even tying double and treble knots. Cat was quite pleased with the threat offered by Caesar and Brutus who growled threateningly whenever either gentleman so much as looked in their direction.

"Very good, Mr. D'Ashley. I am sure that will do quite nicely. Now pull up a chair next to this post. Good. Bind your feet securely to the legs. Excellent. Now I shall just ask you to put your hands behind you." Placing her knife on the floor, Cat set about binding his hands as well. Then, she checked all the knots D'Ashley had made and redoubled them, just to be sure. With sudden inspiration, she fetched a pitcher and carefully poured water over the ropes to tighten them still further.

This accomplished, Cat set about making herself a cup of tea. While she waited for the pot to boil, she took a wet cloth and cleaned the custard off her dogs' faces, much to the outrage of her captives, whose furious profanity she could hear for some time after she had made her way out of the kitchen.

It was still some hours before dawn, and, now that danger was no longer imminent, Cat felt the fatigue of the last several days settle inexorably upon her. Yawning, she decided to get what sleep she could before riding to the village in the morning to inform the magistrate. She took a moment to look in on Audrey, who was still sleeping soundly in the library. Poor girl, she thought, I shall have to do something to set her straight. In spite of her sympathy, however, Cat did take the precaution of locking the library soundly to prevent any intervention on the girl's part. Then she wearily climbed the stairs to her chamber, thinking that it had indeed been a most tiring last two days.

Chapter Eighteen

Upon reaching her own chamber, Cat was filled with a sudden, piercing nostalgia and overwhelming relief. She was home at last. She was drawn toward the window and stood there, candle in hand, contemplating for a time the serene moonlit grounds and the distant glimmer of the sea. So much had happened in the last months that she felt almost a stranger to her former self. Finding herself in these surroundings prompted a longing for the past, so simple and uncomplicated. Meanwhile, Caesar and Brutus seemed wholly unperturbed by their adventures and soon found their way onto her bed with little difficulty. They quickly curled themselves up there and went to sleep as if the terrors of the last thirty-six hours had never taken place.

Cat was finally at leisure to remove her costume, and she did so with a good deal of relief, taking comfort in the simple familiarity of a crisp cotton nightrail. Before snuffing her candle, she bolted her door securely, just in case, and grate-

fully crawled into the lavender-scented eiderdown.
Even though the events of the last two days had
jostled about in her head for several moments, she
nevertheless fell into a deep sleep, accompanied
by the gentle snores of her loyal canine companions.

When Hazelforth and Chumley finally reached
the gates of Sparrowell Hall, they dismounted and
secured their horses quietly; then, crouched low,
they proceeded toward the Hall taking cover in the
shadowy shrubberies. As the silhouette of Sparrowell came into view, the men saw that one of
the rooms on the upper level was lit.

"Look there, Mr. Hazelforth!" Chumley whispered. "That's Miss Cat's chamber."

The two advanced stealthily toward the manor
house, keeping well within the darkened perime-
ters, and taking care to make as little noise as possible. All about them, the night was calm, the
silence broken only by the low hum of crickets.
They were just below the lighted window when
they were rewarded with the sight of Cat herself
who stood on the terrace for a moment holding
her candle, looking out wistfully over the moonlit
landscape. After a short time, she quietly turned
and went inside.

Much relieved to see Cat apparently unharmed,
Hazelforth grasped Chumley by the sleeve and
pulled him down to a crouching position. "It's

clear they have Miss Catherine imprisoned in her room," he whispered. "You must ride into the village and get the magistrates and some men. I shall try to gain the window."

Without further ado, Chumley nodded and disappeared into the darkness, leaving Hazelforth to contemplate his task. Inwardly he blessed whichever of Cat's ancestors had determined to allow stout vines to curl themselves up the sides of the building unchecked. If they were as sturdy as they promised, he should be able to reach Cat's window with very little difficulty. In fact, it seemed a little odd to him, now that he thought about it, that such an enterprising person as Cat had been left to her own devices with such an available means of escape at her disposal. Perhaps, he thought with a furious start, she was not alone.

Although Cat had fallen asleep almost as quickly as her pets, her rest was by no means as untroubled. In the darkness, her brow furrowed as her dreams became progressively nonsensical, replaying all of the events of recent days but, in the annoying manner of such dreams, oddly mixed and sorted. Geoffrey D'Ashley rode about in a curricle pulled by Caesar and Brutus, pursued hotly by Snagworth and Audrey in wedding garments while guests from the costume ball placed bets as to who would reach Vauxhall Gardens first. Then Lady Montrose appeared wearing gossamer wings, floating above the crowd and finally wafting down to where Cat was applying a plaster to Mr. Abelwhite's nose. "Hush," she was saying, "you mustn't make a noise, my dear." Suddenly, it seemed to Cat as if the voice were changing from Lady Montrose's to that of Mr. Hazelforth. What a remarkable dream, she mused hazily, trying to rouse herself.

As Cat pulled herself from the clutches of the dream, she was alarmed to feel the suffocating pressure of a hand over her mouth. Instantly, she began to struggle, but she was held firmly and fast. Her heart raced in a sudden panic. "Hush, my dear," the voice came again. "You must be quiet so I can get you out of here."

It took several seconds for the significance of these words and the voice which spoke them to take hold, but when Cat finally grasped that her captor was the man she loved, she immediately ceased straining against him and instead threw her arms about him. She rested there for some minutes as he clasped her tightly to him, stroking her hair, and not saying a word. Indeed, the unseemliness of their situation bothered neither.

After a time, he released her reluctantly. "Come, Cat," he whispered, kissing her lightly on the forehead. "It is just a few hours until dawn. I must get you away from here before it is light."

By this time, Caesar and Brutus, proving their inadequacy as watchdogs, had roused themselves and begun to bounce about on the bed, wagging their tails and jumping up on Cat and Hazelforth. Impatiently, he hushed them and tried to pull Cat from her bed.

"But, Mr. Hazelforth . . ." she protested, not bothering to whisper.

"Hush, Cat!" he hissed back. "Do you want to bring them down about our ears? Now I fear we must go the way I came, down the vine. Do you think you can manage it?"

"Of course, Mr. Hazelforth," she replied. "I have been climbing down those vines since I was ten years old, but really there's not the slightest need . . ."

"Don't be stubborn, Cat," he whispered urgently. "I am not about to expose you to any further danger. Now come along."

"I am not being stubborn," she began again, "I only want to tell you . . ."

"Tell me when we're away, Cat. Now shall I carry you or will you climb down yourself?"

Cat hesitated a moment longer, wondering whether Mr. Hazelforth would feel even more foolish if she allowed him to force her to scale her own wall unnecessarily after going to some trouble to effect an unnecessary rescue. She almost wished now that she had played the damsel in distress and waited for her savior to arrive. She sighed heavily, recognizing that she had once again failed to fulfill convention's expectations.

Impatiently, Hazelforth swept her into his arms and headed for the window. "I know you dislike my meddling," he whispered in even tones, "but I hope you will understand I want you well out of harm's way before there's any shooting."

"But, Mr. Hazelforth," she returned, hanging her head, "I'm very sorry, but I'm afraid the shooting's already been done. But at least," she added brightly, "I haven't murdered anyone!"

Having left Caesar and Brutus securely locked in her chamber, Cat led Hazelforth down the stairs, first to the library. Much to Cat's chagrin, Audrey was nowhere to be seen and the French doors to the garden stood open. "Oh, dear!" Cat cried, "I do hope she hasn't gone and untied those two!" She quickly crossed to the desk and found there a short note, crudely written.

"Listen to this," she called to Hazelforth. " 'Dear Miss Cat,' " she read, " 'I am mortal sorry for my part in this wickedness and I am going far away for I know that I must hang if I am caught. Tell me mum she was right. I am a sorry girl indeed. Audrey.' "

"I suppose I had best go down and make sure all is well belowstairs," Hazelforth told her with a wry grin. "I hate to have come this far without playing my part in this comedy, however small."

Although Hazelforth had listened to her story with relief and good humor (and, had she known it, a good deal of admiration), Cat decided that it was perhaps best for her to stay where she was and allow him to at least investigate on his own. She curled herself up on the sofa, drifting in and out of sleep until, half an hour later, Hazelforth returned looking most amused.

"You will be interested to find, Cat, that I have been playing nurse to poor Mr. D'Ashley."

"Poor Mr. D'Ashley indeed!" she snorted.

"Yes. It seems your Audrey did not make her escape without spending some time berating the fellow and, finally, knocking him over the head with a heavy piece of crockery. I've managed to stop the bleeding, but he is indeed in sorry shape."

"Good," pronounced Cat. "I hope it shall repay him for a small fraction of the indignities he visited upon poor Caesar and Brutus. But, you know, I am quite worried about Audrey. I know she's done her share of mischief, but I can't help feeling sorry for her at least. If Snagworth and D'Ashley were lured by fabled treasure, at least her motives were less despicable, for I believe she fancied herself in love with that villain."

"So, tell me, Cat," Hazelforth went on, joining her on the sofa, "just what is this treasure I keep hearing about? It seems to have attracted all sorts of unsavory types, from—my young cousins on the day of Cecily's wedding to the churls below."

"Indeed, Mr. Hazelforth," Cat allowed hesitantly, "I am exceedingly mortified to reveal that family secret. It does not speak well for us at all. It seems, however, I must come clean if I am to have any tranquility in life. It is like this. You see, a certain forebear of mine, several generations removed, was a notorious pinch-penny. He wished to cultivate the fields hereabouts, but was loath to pay to have the land cleared. So, I am ashamed to say he caused rumor of a lavish treasure to be spread and put it about that an enormous amount of gold had been buried beneath one of the stumps in the west acreage. Despicable! But the common folk spent many a long night (for their day labor was committed to him as well) uprooting those stumps until the fields were clear. We've always been too ashamed to admit the story publicly, but that's the truth of the treasure of Sparrowell Hall."

"Well, Cat," Hazelforth laughed, "I hope I do not have to fear that penurious tendency in you as well!"

"Indeed, Mr. Hazelforth, if you had seen my last bill from the bookseller, no such thought would ever have occurred to you."

"Cat," he murmured in some exasperation as he gathered her into his arms, "Can you not call me Charles? This 'Mr. Hazelforth' business will never do. We are to be married, after all."

"Oh, yes," she whispered drowsily, snuggling into his arms, "I almost forgot, Mr. Hazelforth. You needn't be burdened with me. I mean to release you from your kind promise."

"And why is that?" he asked softly as she nestled more closely against him and put her weary head onto his accommodating shoulder.

"Because you do not love me, of course," she

answered, as she drifted at last to sleep. Hazelforth shook his head. So that was the way of it. He would not disturb her now, but as soon as she awoke, he would express to her in unmistakable terms the depths of his love for her. He cradled her in his arms and stroked her hair for some time before he, too, succumbed to sleep.

It was thus that the pair was discovered in the morning, not only by Chumley, the county magistrate, and three deputies, but an extremely overwrought Mr. Bagsmith, whose agitation was brought to an even higher pitch by the sight of his client sleeping peacefully in the arms of an unknown gentleman.

"First things first, Chumley," he cried with a furrowed brow and alarming frown. "Fetch Parson Tweedle and we shall see them properly married before we cast the scoundrel into irons."

Cat and Hazelforth by now started up and looked about in some surprise until they recalled the events of the night before. Chumley was explaining hurriedly that the person whose arms were so charmingly engaged was not one of the villains, but a gentleman of some consequence whose efforts had been combined with his own on the previous night.

"That changes very little," Mr. Bagsmith harumphed testily. "Compromise is compromise. The only difference I can possibly see is that he will not be transported after the wedding."

"What a farradiddle!" Cat cried, much put out at his meddling. "Why, we have been sleeping here quite *innocently.*"

"Perhaps *you* have, my love," Hazelforth whispered, "but I fear I cannot own as much myself. My thoughts have been far from innocent."

"Whatever do you mean, Mr. Hazelforth?"

"Surely, my dear, you do not wish me to explain in front of company! Now, Chumley," he went on good-humoredly, "be a good chap and do as Mr. Bagsmith suggests. By all means, go out and find Parson Tweedle at once." Turning to Cat he asked, "You don't mind missing out on a big church wedding do you, my dear?"

"Oh, but Mr. Hazelforth," Cat cried, struggling halfheartedly to extricate herself from his firm embrace, "I vow I had not meant to entrap you thus. I know you do not care for me. Is there no other way, Mr. Bagsmith?"

"Well, Miss Catherine," the solicitor returned with shocked indignation, "I am sure I do not know what that would be!"

"I confess, my dear," Hazelforth told her, tightening his grip, "I must agree with the inestimable Mr. Bagsmith. There really is nothing for it but to be wed."

"But Mr. Hazelforth," she whispered urgently, "I know you do not love me and I am loath to bind you."

Hazelforth, in spite of his deep affection, began to feel the rise of the characteristic exasperation

220

which so many had experienced in their dealings with Cat. "Miss Mansard, for such I will call you until you relent and call me by my Christian name, will you kindly cease your foolishness? It seems then I must say it before all and sundry. I do indeed love you, and I have been bound since the moment I saw you. Is that sufficient?"

"Why, Charles!" she cried with indignation. "Whatever do you mean by loving me all this while and never telling me? Letting me worry myself to tatters over you! Is this the price of propriety, then? That one must suffer in silent throes? If I had a piece of crockery, I should crown you with it as smartly as Audrey did her Mr. D'Ashley!"

"Why then, my Cat, it would be imprudent indeed were I to release you for a single moment from my embrace!"

"But, Charles, I am such a shrew!"

"Do you imagine that I am not equal to your poor tempers? Why, I must tell you that I have sparred with the best at Jackson's parlor."

"Wretch!"

"Ah, Cat! That is what I love about you most! You never disgust me with common civilities!" Turning at last to the assembled gentlemen, who were agape with conspicuous interest, Hazelforth said with some impatience, "The villains are secured in the kitchen below, thanks to this impetuous miss. Pray address your energies and inquiries to them. Now be off and don't return until Chumley's found the parson."

As soon as they were alone, Hazelforth turned his attentions most assiduously to Cat who, after a very nominal show of protest, did not a thing to discourage them. Suddenly, however, she pulled herself from his embrace and cried, "Heavens! How improper this will look! I cannot be married in my nightrail!"

"Why, Cat," Hazelforth laughed, "you need never worry about propriety again. You may be married in Mr. Bagsmith's greatcoat, for aught I care."

"Oh dear," Cat frowned, perching herself on Hazelforth's knee. "You are quite right, Charles. I don't know what came over me. You don't suppose I have become addicted to all this good behavior, do you?"

"There's little fear of that, my love," Hazelforth murmured as he drew her to him, "little fear of that."

FEEL THE FIRE IN CAROL FINCH'S ROMANCES!

BELOVED BETRAYAL (2346, $3.95)

Sabrina Spencer donned a gray wig and veiled hat before blackmailing rugged Ridge Tanner into guiding her to Fort Canby. But the costume soon became her prison—the beauty had fallen head over heels in love!

LOVE'S HIDDEN TREASURE (2980, $4.50)

Shandra d'Evereux felt her heart throb beneath the stolen map she'd hidden in her bodice when Nolan Elliot swept her out onto the veranda. It was hard to concentrate on her mission with that wily rogue around!

MONTANA MOONFIRE (3263, $4.95)

Just as debutante Victoria Flemming-Cassidy was about to marry an oh-so-suitable mate, the towering preacher, Dru Sullivan flung her over his shoulder and headed West! Suddenly, Tori realized she had been given the best present for a bride: a night of passion with a real man!

THUNDER'S TENDER TOUCH (2809, $4.50)

Refined Piper Malone needed bounty-hunter, Vince Logan to recover her swindled inheritance. She thought she could coolly dismiss him after he did the job, but she never counted on the hot flood of desire she felt whenever he was near!